Praise for *Close is Fine*

The gleeful destruction of this collection's first pages is an early warning that you're entering a world like no other. Not just a world where a car battery might be thrown through a storm window for fun, but one where "I think I have issues with your thought process" is usually meant as a kind of compliment. The stories of *Close Is Fine* could not be so funny if they weren't also so sad, and their energy is always tempered by a narration of sharp reflection and clear, sure-footed prose. This is what I admire most about the book—the tension between the intelligence and control of the storytelling and the mistakes, the lack of control in the actions of the characters he tells us about. These are consistently provocative stories, stories of a very high order.
— Peter Rock, author of *My Abandonment*

"The stories in *Close Is Fine* are a rare treat: vivid and voice-driven, sometimes hilarious and often heartbreaking, with surprising perceptions on every page. Whether they live on dilapidated farms whose wells have been poisoned by pesticides, or play on sports teams named for the local paper mill, or have affairs with soldiers' wives and help friends build replica Howitzers out of scrap wood, Eliot Treichel's characters are all complexly flawed and deeply human. In the bleakness of small-town, rural life, Treichel discovers both horror and humor, degradation and dignity, grief and grace."
— Scott Nadelson, author of *Aftermath* and *Saving Stanley: The Brickman Stories*

"I've been a fan of Treichel's fiction for years; but this book exceeded all my expectations. *Close Is Fine* is a beautiful, big-hearted, and hilarious collection. It features firemen, handymen, bear-wrestlers, and noble barflies, all doing the best they can. Treichel's stories wander the fields, forests, and small towns of the Midwest like an Elizabethan balladeer: steadily amassing the vital, oft-ignored literature of the ninety-nine percent."
— Tyler McMahon, author of *How the Mistakes Were Made*

This splendid collection of stories is part thrill-ride, part ethnographic field study, and part love song, filled with Wisconsin firemen, lumberjacks, pining lovers, wrestling bears, Native American revolutionaries, eloquent philanderers, [and] downtrodden soccer teams. Eliot Treichel is a master ventriloquist, able to summon and sustain an amazing range of voices, and to let his characters tell their glorious and surprisingly wise stories with their own idiosyncratic eloquence.
— K.L. Cook, author of *Love Songs for the Quarantined* and *Last Call*

Close
Is
Fine

CLOSE IS FINE

STORIES

eliot treichel

Close Is Fine

© 2012 Eliot Treichel

ISBN13: 978-1-932010-45-9

Ooligan Press
Portland State University
Department of English
PO Box 751
Portland, Oregon 97207
503.725.9748; 503.725.3561 fax
www.ooliganpress.pdx.edu
ooligan@ooliganpress.pdx.edu

Printed in the United States of America
Cover design by Tristen Jackman
Interior design by Jesse Snavlin

☙

"There are terrible places in this world, but people know
our names there, so we return" on page 18 courtesy of
Russel Dillon, from the poem "Collect Call from the Hague"

ACKNOWLEDGEMENTS

I AM DEEPLY indebted to the following people for their mentorship, support, and inspiration: First thanks must go to the dedicated students and staff at Ooligan Press, with special shout-outs to Rachel Haag, Irene Costello, Kristen Svenson, and Abbey Gaterud. A big thank you to Melanie Bishop, who changed my life. Thanks to Kenny Cook. Thank you Maria Flook, Rick Moody, Amy Hempel, Susan Cheever, and Mary-Beth Hughes, who all read the very earliest versions of this book and helped give it life. More thanks: Liesl Schwabe. William Cambier. Jennifer Goyette. Jackie Melvin. Thank you to the literary journals who first published many of these stories. My gratitude to Rob Spillman, Dorothy Allison, and the Tin House Writer's Workshop. Russell Dillon, Paul Mazza, Christopher Salerno, and Lacy Simons—always. My friends and colleagues at Lane Community College. And most importantly, Shannon and Josephine (and our dog, Summit) for the believing and the love and the innumerable ways you put up with me—from the bottom of my heart.

For Mom & Dad

The following stories were previously published:
"GOOD POTATO SOIL" *Cold-drill*, 2007
"PAPERMAKER PRIDE" *Dos Passos Review*, 2007
"ON BY" *Southern Indiana Review*, 2009
"THE GOLDEN TORCH" *Passages North*, 2009
"CLOSE IS FINE" *CutBank*, 2010
"WERE NOT THAT" *Alligator Juniper*, 2010
"STARGAZER" *Narrative Magazine*, 2011

Contents

"Little rivers, beautiful, wild, and clear, meander through my dreams."
Sigurd F. Olson, *Of Time and Place*

"…in fact it is all wealth, though it resembles the meanest poverty."
Glenway Wescott, *Goodbye, Wisconsin*

Good Potato Soil

THEN DUDE AND I went down into the old barn foundation and broke stuff. We sought out every scrap of glass just so we could hear it shatter. There was a garbage bag full of empties and we pitched them at the wall. Dude shot-putted a car battery through a storm window. Our laughs were like the splinters of glass in our hair, clear and sharp and dangerous.

We took turns batting with a golf club, and we knocked bottles and light bulbs and mason jars into the sunset. Our swings were sometimes miles off, and we'd hear the club cutting through the air. Other times we hit square on, and the impact of it hurt our hands. Sometimes the glass exploded into dust. Sometimes it only split apart in a few chunks, and then we'd pick up the pieces and pitch them again.

Later I found a bowling ball in a small, metal bucket. I dumped the ball out, then set it on top of the wall and climbed after. At the edge of Tatro's field, irrigation sprinklers sprayed arcs of water into long, white feathers. The horizon looked just like the cover of *Houses of the Holy* with the tint dial maxed, the color knob cranked red. One star dotted the sky. A deer tested the open.

Below me, Dude worked through a heap of old shoes with a piece of copper piping. I watched him poke, lift, smell. I grabbed the bowling ball and slung it at him.

"Dude!" I yelled.

The ball hit the concrete and stopped—didn't bounce, didn't roll, didn't move at all. It sounded just like clucking your tongue on the roof of your mouth, only seismic. It landed right where he'd been standing. The bowling ball stopped, and it sort of stopped Dude and me, at least the fun of wrecking things.

"Dude," he said.

After the barn, we went and sat on the balcony of the farmhouse. The balcony was right off our bedroom. We had some lawn chairs, and Dude lit a candle to keep the mosquitoes away. We got high up there a lot, in our plastic chairs. Sometimes, like today, we brought a Styrofoam cooler of beer, though we never bothered with ice.

From the balcony, Dude and I could see over the row of white pines that surrounded our yard and divided us from the potatoes. Beginning just after our yard, the soil was tilled and planted and sprayed for hundreds of acres. To the north, where the highway turned uphill and returned to the woods, a small break led down to the irrigation pump at the river. There was some first-year sorghum and some corn, but the rest was all good potato soil.

"Officially," I said to Dude, lifting my bottle, "the barn is my new favorite game."

Dude slouched in his chair. His hair and beard were the color of dried tobacco, and he wore a ponytail that nearly reached the middle of his back. "You played well," he said, tipping his beer toward me. We had both been wearing the same t-shirts for days, which is how a summer should go.

I'm telling you, that sunset would not end. I pointed at an airplane's silent dash, but Dude didn't see.

"We can always find more," he said, looking at the empty road.

Dude and I hadn't been up to the roof of the house in a long time, not since the night we'd gotten Ruben's note, so we decided to go up. A shingle had come loose from its tack. Three nails that were manufactured in 1922 held the eave. These were places where we had to stick our hands and feet. The pitch was steep, set for a climate of bad, heavy winters. In truth, the hardest part was coming back down.

Dude and I perched ourselves next to the chimney and faced the old barn. The pit had darkened, but a faint band of light still stretched across the horizon. We found a dead bat plastered against the chimney, its body dried, wings spread. Dude peeled it away, all except for the black sticky parts that wouldn't come up. We guessed that the bat had been electrocuted; lightning rods were set the length of the house. I thought, well, that's how fast lightning probably is, though what I've come to learn is that you can see most things coming from a long ways off. When Dude dropped the bat down the chimney, we never heard it reach the bottom.

We hadn't gone to visit Ruben yet. That last time we crawled to the rooftop, Dude and I had spent the first part of the night playing darts at the tavern. Besides Granny the bartender, Dude and I were the only ones at the Stargazer. When Granny was doing other things, we served ourselves and kept all our quarters for the board. I couldn't hit a triple but once. When we'd finally made it home, every light in the house was out, the inside as dark as the moonless night. We found the note on top of Dude's pillow, written on a yellow notepad. Ruben's handwriting looked clean, more comfortable than I'd thought it'd look on paper.

> *Boys—*
> *I failed my piss test and they're taking me to jail.*
> *My sister will get more of my stuff.*
> *Please watch my dog.*
> *—R*

After the note, we went up to the roof, and we didn't see a thing in all that distance. Dude clenched a hand around a lightning rod. He curved out his chest and laid back his head, begging lightning to ground right through him. "Take me!" he cried that night. Reaching out his other arm, not a cloud around, he said, "Oh, sweet Lord, take me!"

THE OTHER PLACE we hung out was Michelle's playroom. Michelle was Ruben's daughter, who he didn't have custody of. But she had a Nintendo, which meant we had a Nintendo, and so we hung out in her playroom a lot. Plastic wrap covered the windows, and through them the yard looked as if we were living in an empty gallon of milk.

Dude and I always played this off-road car game we'd found at the Goodwill in Antigo. I'd just recaptured the lead and was doing everything

I could to hold Dude off. We sat in school desks made for grade-school size bodies, Dude with a joint between his lips. The landscape of the utility carpeting was ranged with coloring books and snapped crayons. A mess of play toys circled us. Figures from board games were scattered everywhere. A giant, orange rabbit looked over my shoulder. Somehow, I felt stuck.

My car skipped around a corner, Dude bumping me against the outside hay bales. He hit my back tires, trying to push me into a spin. He leaned his desk into mine, so I leaned back.

With my last burst, I tried to cut Dude off. Then he flipped me end-over-end with his car, and that was it. He crossed with the checkered flag, while I landed with an upside-down explosion.

Dude used the bonus points from his win to stack the quality of his tires. He was a firm believer in good tread. I was all engine, all suspension.

I'd lived in the house since ice-out, but I'd never even heard Ruben mention Michelle by name. A few photos of her hung in the upstairs hall. Dude thought she was in like second or third grade. He once kissed Michelle's mom just before passing out on her when Ruben was in jail the first time.

One night during an early summer party, I heard Ruben screwing in Michelle's room. As much as I'd thought I liked Ruben, as much as he seemed legendary to me, more than anything else he was someone I didn't want to be.

That afternoon, hours before anyone arrived for our little fiesta, hours before I heard him having sex, Ruben walked up the driveway with a package of hamburger meat and half a six-pack left on the ring.

He'd taken to calling us his boys. The thing about Ruben was his eyes, which were the kind of pale blue that was nearly colorless. The depth of Ruben's eyes just sort of went on, and when a person looked at him level they looked back into the animal part of man. He had salt-and-pepper hair, and he kept his mustache trimmed neat. The whole time I'd lived with Dude and him, Ruben had talked about these friends, these girls from East Moline, and that he'd get them to come up and show us everything.

Dude and I were sitting on the trunk of the Chrysler, failing to tele-pathically communicate with one another.

"Boys," Ruben said. "How are my boys?"

Ruben had to catch his breath a little. He worked at the trout pond in Elkton and sometimes fish reek poured off him. "Tell you what," he said, splitting the beers between us. "Just don't go running to your mommies."

We tried to say, "No problem."

As the grill heated, the three of us drove the old lawn mower around the front yard for kicks. I played chicken with a shrub and scratched my face. Dude cut random swatches of grass, crop circles of his very own. Ruben rode the mower up on two wheels around a corner. Then he cooked the meat perfectly, and he even fried some onions and added a little black pepper to them. Ruben let us use paper plates, let us take a clean one for each burger, and we felt like kings.

After we ate, Ruben's brother showed up. He looked nothing like Ruben, was dark-skinned and dark-eyed, and I couldn't think of much to say to him. I stacked a fire in the pit, waiting to light it because the bugs weren't out yet. Ruben drove the lawn mower around back with his brother riding on the hood, legs dangling over the front. Ruben pulled up so close that Dude and I had to step back, and then he engaged the blade for effect a couple times. He made his brother pour us all a drink, and I shot mine straight, making sure Ruben saw.

By the time the friends from Illinois arrived, I'd lost a great deal of coordination. Except for the coloring, one a redhead and one a brunette, the girls had nearly the same hair—straight and long and with fluffy, curled bangs. They looked pale and hungry, closer to Ruben's age than mine. In a way, they seemed the plainest-looking women I'd ever seen. In fact, they were gorgeous. Their jeans were tight and the laces to their high-tops untied. Their bra straps slipped out from under their tank tops. Ruben hugged and kissed each one, making both of them smile. It was easy to see we were the boys. He introduced Dude and me with something funny and a little exaggerated, trying to create an impression.

I mumbled to the girls, "What's up?"

Ruben's nostalgia was some of the best drinking music I'd heard. We all listened and laughed, and one of the girls rubbed his shoulders as he talked. It wasn't really the facts that made his tales so special, it was the tone of his storytelling. His voice was harsh from thousands of cigarettes, but Ruben made whatever he did sound beautiful, no matter how many died in the crash. I was young then, but I knew that's what a poet did.

After Dude went to bed, and everyone else went to the Stargazer, I stayed in the backyard. For a long time, I sat and bulldozed the white-hot coals in the fire. My spine seemed like it wanted to run down the highway without me. I pulled grass up from the lawn, tossing handfuls into the fire to see them smoke and disappear. The crickets and tree frogs seemed like some kind of sonar I couldn't understand. I woke up in the house, with no idea how I made it there.

A steady, repetitive squeaking woke me up. I heard a woman moan. Next to my bed, the wall was knocking. Every now and then, I'd hear Ruben. I whispered to Dude, but he slept through it all. The woman panted and moaned and begged. When it was over, the silence was its own kind of unbearable noise.

I stayed up, sweating out the night, watching the sky brighten. Later, I got up to take a leak from the balcony. I'd already started by the time I noticed them. Off in the yard, Ruben and the brunette—naked, hand in hand, out cold—weighed down the hammock so that it nearly touched the ground.

The next morning Ruben made us all Bloody Marys. Nine in the morning and he was wired on all systems go, springing around the kitchen, cutting celery, whistling. Dude wore a pair of aviator sunglasses. He'd made toaster waffles and was looking in the fridge for the margarine. He started getting really upset because he'd just bought a whole tub.

"Here," Ruben said, holding out a five-dollar bill.

In the Stargazer, the walls were covered with dollar bills upon dollar bills that patrons had written things on and then left for the collection. It was a recent tradition. Dude and I had a couple up there. There were a few big bills, a fifty, more tens, some twenties.

Dude's mouth made an almost perfect circle. "This is from us," Ruben said, nodding at his girl. "For last night." He turned the money so I could read. BUTTER IS BETTER. The sheets in Michelle's room haven't been changed since.

Dude and I played again. We played Nintendo another two hours, until our mouths were dry and our tongues were like the sticky side of duct tape. We always split everything, halfsies, so we called it a draw.

We drove to the Stargazer. I held my arm out the passenger window, slipstreaming it through the wind, ready to buy the first drafts—a dollar bill that read WE MISS YOU in my pocket.

THE LETTER MICHELLE handed me was written on the same notepad that Ruben had used. When I looked close enough, I could see the imprint of Ruben's pen on Michelle's letter, and if only her mom had looked as close as she needed to maybe she would've seen that Ruben wasn't around anymore. Or maybe she did notice, and that's exactly why she up and left Michelle with only a gym bag of clothes and a toothbrush in our living room.

"What is this?" I asked Michelle.

I said, "Your dad isn't here."

I yelled for Dude, even though I knew he was still in the fields.

Michelle just stood there, not saying a thing, looking at me like the dog did after getting left out all night. Michelle wore a yellow dress, white stockings, and white shoes, as if it was school-photo day. Her hair was long and frizzy. She smelled like bubble gum and the way she stood there silently, staring back, was impossible.

It's your turn for a while. She likes to watch cartoons when they're on.

That's all it said, yet I read the instructions over and over, as if they would suddenly say something more helpful.

When I sat down on the couch, Michelle sat down on the other end. It had been another heavy, humid day. The living room stayed shaded, and it was a nice place to sit and unwind after so many hours of being in the sun.

The room was silent, and so was the land outside. There was a streak of light that showed how much was in the air. Out of the corner of my eye, I could see that Michelle was still looking at me. I smelled horrible, like labor and pesticide and dirt. I crossed my arms, and from the reflection on the television I saw that she was doing the same. There we were, side by side, made smaller in the reflection coming off that huge old Zenith. We were two kids really, and she was on summer vacation just like my mind. Dude and I also loved cartoons. We could all just watch cartoons,

I thought. At the same time, I understood then that I was going to fuck it all up royally.

I rotated the antenna all over the place, but all I could get in was a soap opera.

"Have you seen this before?" I asked her.

Michelle shrugged her shoulders.

"Okay," I said, "well, this is a really good show. It's not a cartoon, but it's still pretty decent. I think you'll like it. So you just sit here, and I'll be right back," I told her, probably like every adult in her life had told her, and then I went upstairs and got out the shoebox and went on the balcony to collect myself.

❦

THERE WAS ALSO our kitchen. In a bottom drawer of the refrigerator, a bag of Red Delicious apples rotted in an inch of pink water. Our sink was filled with dishes and remnants of past meals like tuna fish sandwiches. The dishes were stacked and piled so it was hard to get a cup under the faucet. Michelle had to stand on a chair to reach. Only one burner on the stove worked, and there was a pan of chicken bones that we never took out of the oven. The floor was covered by dried spills and dog hair. Mouse shit dotted the shelves.

Dude and I had it figured so we were barely home at all, leaving the Westinghouse to ferment itself, the dog to run wherever. With Michelle there, we pretty much kept it the same way. When we were forced to cook at home, we only washed the one pot and one knife we needed. The one plate, one fork, each. Most mornings, Dude and I bought a box of stale doughnuts and then left a few for Michelle. We usually just went in the woods during lunch. Sometimes we forgot to come home after work and went straight to the Stargazer and ate and drank until Granny made us leave. When we got home, the tv would always be on, and Michelle would be on the couch. Most often she was asleep, curled up with the blanket off her bed.

We'd carry her upstairs and tuck her in, and sometimes I'd just stare at her. "Sweet dreams," I'd whisper in her ear, hoping it could somehow make a difference.

A FEW WEEKS after Michelle moved in, a letter about the house's well water showed up in the mail. We didn't even know we'd been well tested. We weren't sure whether the positives meant good or bad, but it was the latter. The letter advised the pregnant and nursing to drink bottled water because of the pesticides. Dude just kept using the tap, saying he couldn't taste anything different than any other water he'd ever had. I sort of just stopped drinking water, unless I was at the Stargazer. We started buying twelve-packs of soda for Michelle and told her to drink more pop.

We had an old washer and dryer, so Dude and I and Michelle had mostly clean clothes, though we stored them in piles on the floor. In the bathroom, the shower drain was green as moss in the river. We were always out of toilet paper. Utility bills waited past due, and the mutt got low on chow.

But we had good nights. Some nights the three of us would all sit on the couch and eat pizza and watch tv. Marley, as we'd renamed the dog, would buddy up with Michelle. We'd sit with the lights out and we'd get a nice breeze through the windows. If it was real muggy, we'd run a fan. Dude and I would take turns sneaking upstairs to the balcony. Hours later we'd reach a point where we were laughing so hard our stomachs hurt, and then we'd realize we were hungry.

"I want candy!" Dude would scream, tickling Michelle in the ribs.

"Candy!" I'd yell, egging her on more.

We'd keep going until we'd get Michelle screaming, "I want candy! Get me candy!" Dude or I would drive to the gas station and buy candy bars, and bags of chips, and more pop, and then we'd make a great pile of it in front of the couch, and the three of us would forget everything else except for the tastes we were tasting.

Those nights on the couch were some of the only times Michelle really talked with us. Besides sneaking upstairs, we didn't keep much else hidden. It was too hard not to curse in front of her, and eventually she started in with it. We'd ask her what she'd done during the day, and she'd tell us how she'd watched tv, or taken some of her toys outside and played in the driveway. Marley took her on long walks in the fields. Mostly, we didn't listen to her. She'd talk a lot about her mom, how her mom was coming back, or how she wished her mom would never return. When Dude asked Michelle if her mom had a boyfriend, she told Dude to shut his trap. It was the closest we got to speaking about Ruben with her. Once Michelle said that she wished we were dead, and another time she drew a nice picture of us—Marley, Michelle, Dude, and me, standing in front of our house, waving.

❧

LEONARD, OUR DEALER, came by for the Fourth of July, which was also Dude's birthday. After we shut Michelle in her playroom, we all went up to the balcony and exchanged gifts. My present to Dude was a paper sack full of bottle rockets. "My friend," I said, handing him the fireworks. "From me."

We aimed over the pine trees, sending the fireworks into the fields. Dude lit some and hurled them straight up, as if they were batons. Some cruised off toward the potatoes, others toward the house. We tried to hit cars. Not enough cars drove by, so we started aiming at Marley.

We always tried to miss. As the fireworks whistled past him, Marley would run off. Once they'd crashed into the lawn, he'd turn and charge them, barking louder than their screech. Marley would bite at them, the sparks stinging his snout, until the bottle rockets popped and he sprang backwards.

"Hey," Dude said, slowly. He said, "This isn't funny," which made all three of us laugh even harder.

"It's all fun and games," Leonard added. He fired a bottle rocket at the lawn mower, and it thunked off the side. Marley went after it, and I fished out a beer and leaned against the deck railing. A brown car moved up the highway, so I called it out.

"We've got a vehicle," Dude said.

As the car moved closer, it began to slow.

Leonard had another bottle rocket in one hand, his lighter in the other. "Permission to fire?" he asked. He had closed one eye so he could aim better. The bottle rocket swayed, if only slightly, on its thin red stick. The car was brown, square, domestic. None of us knew who it belonged to.

"Countdown," I began.

It was going to be a bull's-eye. It'd be beautiful. It'd be the funniest thing yet.

"Abort!" Dude yelled. "Abort! Abort!"

Dude had only met Ruben's parole officer once before, right after Ruben went back in. I wasn't home, and Dude told the guy we hardly even knew Ruben, which was sort of true, because we hardly knew anything at all.

Leonard threw the bottle rocket off the porch, and it screamed into the front yard. Marley was also screaming, as was my head. Leonard started to help Dude stash things, and I tried to stop on one thought.

"I'll light incense," I said, and walked around in circles.

The car had pulled up next to the house. I stood perfectly still, listening, waiting for the sound of walkie-talkies. Leonard and Dude were gone. I grabbed the sheets off my bed and went and got down in the closet.

Breathe, I finally had to tell myself.

Then there was laughing. Leonard and Dude were laughing in the living room.

Through the crack between the door and its frame, I watched Dude walk into our bedroom. He moved out to the balcony and then straight back into the room, looking around and calling my name as the screen door slammed shut behind him.

"Dude," I whispered from my spot.

Dude glanced up at the ceiling. He had no idea where I was. I heard the engine start up, then the gravel of the driveway as the car drove off. "Wasn't him," he said, grinning. Two old sisters who'd grown up in the house had just wanted to see who was living there. When the sisters asked if they could come inside, Dude said our dad didn't allow strangers.

"They asked about the barn," Dude said, "and I told them we lost it in a windstorm."

I walked out of the closet and looked at him. His eyes were slits of peppermint, and he was standing so that he seemed to be falling backwards. I looked at the wall behind him, and everything beyond that, all the way to the river. How exactly did the place look those days? There are terrible places in this world, but people know our names there, so we return.

❦

I sat alone on the roof of the farmhouse with my back against the chimney and the sack of leftover fireworks in my lap. A tractor, headlights on, headed down the road. To the east, a tar-black sky.

That afternoon, Dude and I had gone into Antigo to visit Ruben. We had to add oil to the car each way. We wanted to tell him about Michelle.

A shield of security glass separated Ruben from us. He wore an orange jumpsuit and white slippers. Several phones without dials hung in the rooms. Dude and I each took a receiver. Ruben used two to hear us, one on each side of his head.

Ruben's eyes seemed different—not broken, but less there. It was strange, looking through that glass window. Both rooms were nearly identical, and if it wasn't for the jumpsuit, it would have been hard to tell which side was which. I mainly nodded and confirmed and tried to show my support by just being there. Ruben asked about his dog. Dude said he was happy as ever. We didn't tell him we were feeding Marley sliced cheese because there was nothing else left.

Ruben wanted to know about work and if anyone had called. We saw him for maybe ten minutes, and we were too skittish to say anything about Michelle, or his sister never showing, or suspect levels of nitrates in the drinking water. When Ruben asked me what was new, I said, "You know, it's all good."

Outside, Dude unlocked the car. His windshield was thick with bugs. "You got to feel for the guy," he said.

"You got to feel lucky we're not him." I wanted to lighten the mood.

"That's certainly it," he said. "Capital L, lucky."

Up on the roof, I launched the last of the rockets. I lit all the fuses, counted to three, and then I threw them. For a moment, as they fell, the fireworks were silent. Then the rockets spiraled off in trails, until they exploded: brightly, quickly, a flash.

On the ride home from the jail, Dude and I made a pact to clean the kitchen, but now I didn't want to come down. The situation was beyond us. It was moist, and stagnant. It's funny how things change, the way putrid fruit smells from one day to another. When we'd moved in, Ruben walked on air, and the kitchen made us want to eat.

I stuffed the paper bag down the chimney. Our phone had already been disconnected. It wouldn't be long before the power got shut off. The propane would be the only thing left. The night suddenly seemed as if I couldn't hear things right, like that silence after hearing someone fucking.

After we'd tucked Michelle in, while the northern lights shimmered above us, Dude and I went and rested on the walls of the barn foundation. Glowing sheets of green rippled over the night like water reflections on a black-bottomed lake. "Dude," I said, thinking then, under that incredible sky, that it was finally the right time to stop. "Do you ever see things," I asked, "that maybe aren't really there?"

"No," he said, reaching a finger up toward the lights. "They're usually there."

We'd finally bagged the mess of our kitchen. We'd cleared everything, the dirty plates, every cup, all the food-encrusted cookware. Even if it wasn't spoiled, or wrecked, or ours, it all got put in trash bags and moved to the top of the barn wall. That was what we had—a warm summer night, and some moment of starlight and will.

Dude stood, and paced atop the wall. "Tell me!" he shouted to the potatoes. He folded his hands together, lifting them above his head, as if in prayer, or cuffs. What had died long ago, we were only seeing now. "Is there anyone out there?"

The next morning, I'd go get doughnuts with Dude, and I'd work another day, and then we'd come home powdered in dirt, and that would be the last time. I once told Dude that whatever happened, he'd get the Nintendo, and I'd get the dog. In reality, I would steal the car and leave him everything else, including Michelle.

Alternating turns, Dude and I started to chuck our crap. Dude grabbed a bag and swung it back and forth, going for height and not distance. When the sack hit, we heard a *boing* from the toaster oven, heard plates and glasses breaking.

We devised a game where we tried to make two bags collide in mid-air. Dude even set up a point system. One of my bags slipped and flew off, nearly clobbering him. I thought for sure I'd won, but he had some moves.

"If you knock someone out," I argued, "you should get a bonus."

As the night went on, the columns of light turned from green to white to green again. Dude and I each had only one thing left to throw. He held the base of a blender, and I was down to a shelf from the refrigerator.

Dude took the end of the power cord and began swinging the blender so fast that it whistled. I imagined the cord snapping, the heavy base flying right into the side of my head. I wanted to cover myself, but I wanted to watch Dude send the thing even more.

The blender tumbled through the air, the cord trailing a half-turn slower, and then it dropped like a bird hit with shot. It crashed a mile from the barn and rolled toward the field.

"A million points if I hit it!" I yelled.

With a quick wind-up, I hurled the glass shelf in the direction of the blender. It sounded good when it hit, but I had misfired—halfsies, nowhere near.

THE OLD DOG had been leading Mary to the river when it stopped and pinned its nose to the ground. Mary whistled at him as she strode past. "Jiggs," she said, "let's go."

Jiggs spun circles and started pawing a hole in the dirt. He had a thin, speckled coat—brown and gray and white—and ears that flopped over. His growl kept strangers away. He jammed his nose in the loose earth, then sniffed and huffed and sneezed. When Mary finally quit walking, she tried to make her voice sound as stern as her father's, which rarely had to ask Jiggs to do anything twice.

"Jiggs," she yelled, "Come!" She was only nine.

Jiggs didn't move. His tail simply whipped back and forth, and he barked and snapped at the air. He used his snout to scoop dirt from his hole. He was crouched low, resting on his front legs, pushing his nose through the soil.

"Here!" Mary shouted, stomping a foot in the grass. "Jesus," she said, and felt bad, even though no one else heard.

For a second, Jiggs froze. Then he jumped up and began rotor-tilling the ground, spraying soil between his back legs. The bits of dirt and gravel landing in the field sounded like rain pittering against a window. Mary marched back toward him and noticed that he now had something in his mouth. He gulped whatever it was in two quick bites. He was always finding horse poop to eat.

Mary pulled at Jiggs's collar, which he leaned into heavily. "Knock it off," she said, and swatted his rear. She was thinking of how bad his breath would be. When she finally saw what he had, Mary pulled so hard his collar slipped over his head. "Go on," she yelled, kicking at him, the empty O of rope swinging in her hand. She landed a foot good enough that he'd yelped.

The mice were pink and hairless, hardly as big as her thumb. Their eyes hadn't even opened, and they squirmed blindly together in the bottom of the nest, coated with dirt. Before she could stop him, Jiggs swooped in and snatched one more.

"Stop," Mary screamed. "Git! Go!" She kicked at him harder but missed.

The mouse bodies crunched as Jiggs chewed. Mary chased after him, screaming, waving her arms. Jiggs cut back and forth, tore around the field in big circles, too fast for her. When she fell and skinned her elbows, Jiggs went for another mouse. She caught up to him at the nest and whipped him on the butt as hard she could. She scared herself by how much her hand stung.

Mary knelt in the grass, straddling over the last two mice. Jiggs lay only a few feet away. "Don't you dare," she said, whenever he moved, even a little. Her voice had thickened with mucus. The scrapes on her arms stung, and she'd ripped a hole in her good jeans. She wasn't supposed to be playing in her good jeans.

One of the mice was already dead, the tail end of its body gone. It made her think of a worm caught in the hot sun, drying out, shriveling. The second mouse was trying to crawl somewhere. Mary scooped it up and used the end of her shirt to make a little pouch. Delicately, by a front leg, she lifted the dead mouse and added it to her nest, just so Jiggs wouldn't get it.

Mary started back for home, and Jiggs went right to the hole. When he didn't find anything, he came charging up the low, steady hill. Anytime he tried to get at the bundle, Mary swung her leg at him and told him what a horrible, no-good dog he was, and how she hated him.

THE GRIME ON the windows in the feed room diffused the sun, but Mary didn't want to turn on the light. She'd made a little spot for the mice in the top of a hay bale. She peeled a flake off another bale and covered the mice with it, hoping her father, or Vin, the farm hand, wouldn't set anything atop them, or stand on them, or crush them some other way. Then she dragged Jiggs to his doghouse and chained him to his post. She went to the spigot and cupped her palm and filled it with water. She walked quickly so the water wouldn't all drip through her fingers.

Outside, Jiggs was howling. The mouse wouldn't drink, couldn't drink without an eyedropper or something, so Mary just poured the water over it and tried to wash off some of the grit stuck to its skin.

The mouse felt cold, and had turned pale. Mary wrapped her hands around it, and promised she'd keep it safe. She imagined the mouse warming instantly, but she couldn't tell if it made any difference. She pretended her hand was a small oven, that it was a heavy jacket, that it was a heating lamp, just like the ones they used to keep the chicks happy at the feed store. She wasn't sure how long she sat like that, but it was long enough to forget where she was. She heard someone coming.

Mary hid the mice and went in the house. Her grandmother was the only other person inside. Nanna was blind, and she didn't stray far from the living room. She spent whole days sitting in her chair by the bay window. Just feeling the warmth on her face, she once said to Mary, was almost like seeing outside.

Mary tried to sneak past, but Nanna caught her. "Sweetie," she called out. "What was all that barking?"

Mary went and stood next to her grandmother and took one of her hands. Mary and Nanna faced the window, which opened onto the front yard. Mary noticed a spot of blood on the front of her own shirt. She looked out at the lawn and the gravel turnaround. There was a vacant flagpole and a deer statue and a gigantic blue spruce clustered in the middle of it all, bordered by white decorative rock. Jiggs had stopped and gone into his doghouse, but his head was poking out, his eyes fixed on the empty road.

"He rolled in something bad," Mary said. "I was spraying him with the hose."

Nanna sniffed. "He sounded miserable."

"I hope he learned his lesson."

As Nanna's blindness got more severe, she often had Mary name things for her. Nanna would shuffle around the living room, her eyes open, but cloudy and broken, searching with her hands, pointing at things, picking things up—sometimes dropping them, or knocking them over—asking, "Sweetie, what's this? What's this, sweetie? What's this?"

An ashtray, Mary would say. That's the remote. A shelf. The lamp cord. This is a newspaper. A magazine. This is the afghan. Our Bible. That's my stomach. My cheek. A picture, Mary would say, the only one left of her mother. That's your daughter.

Now Nanna patted the back of Mary's hand. Mary noticed how thin her grandmother's skin appeared. Except for a few long white hairs, Nanna was nearly bald. "Tell me about the river," Nanna said.

Mary didn't mention the mice. All those times Nanna had asked what something was, when she picked something up, when she pointed, Mary always told the truth. She wanted to tell Nanna, but Mary was afraid she'd done something wrong. "I saw a snapping turtle," Mary lied. "He plopped off a log and into the water. And then he just floated there. Just the tip of his nose above the surface."

Nanna smiled. "Your grandpa used to grab them up and scare me," she said. "He'd wave them in my face and then run after me and tell me they were going to bite, just so he could get me to scream."

❧

SOMEONE RAPPED ON Mary's door. She knew it was her father. She thought he was going to ask her to help cook dinner.

"Get your shoes," he said. "I want to show you something." He took her out to the barn, down the long aisle of empty stalls and to the hay room. He turned on the big overhead light, which sputtered and then hummed. When he lifted off the flake of hay, the mice were still there—the second almost dead now.

He didn't even have to ask if she had done it. "I'm sorry," she blurted out.

"Oh, Mare," her father said when he saw the tears coming.

Mary's father said he was sorry that she'd seen Jiggs being a dog, but she shouldn't have brought the mice. "Mice spread," he explained. "We don't want them in the barn. They'll eat through the feed. That's why we have cats." Besides, he explained, a mouse needs its mother. Someone to keep it warm, to nurse it, to teach it how to be a mouse. "We're not that," her father said.

She almost asked, "Why not?"

"I know you wanted to help," her father went on, "but once Jiggs started, you should have just let him finish."

❧

MARY AND HER father stood on the porch after dinner. She wore light blue jammies dotted with soccer balls and basketballs and baseballs. Her father had promised to walk the mouse back into the field and find a good place for it and set it free. "They were living in a little hollow spot," she said.

"A den," her father replied. "They call it a den. I promise I'll find a good area. And then I'll come tuck you in." He got down on a knee so she could kiss him on the cheek, just like she did every night. He put an arm around her and pulled her in for a reluctant hug.

It was nearly dark out, though the underbellies of the clouds were lit red. The late light changed the color of the lawn and the pastures, and to Mary it all looked purple. "Okay, bedtime," her father said, though usually she stayed up longer. "Say goodnight to Nanna, and then you get between those sheets."

Mary lingered, watching her father head toward the barn. Up ahead, Jiggs stood at the end of his chain, his tail wagging a slow, full cadence.

Mary's father turned and looked back at her, but didn't stop walking. "I mean it," he said. "You get off to bed."

When he disappeared around the corner of the barn, she finally went in. She ran down the hallway, past the living room and the bedrooms, and to the bathroom. She put the toilet lid down and then stood on it so she could see out the small window that faced the back of the barn. Besides the one in her father's room, it was the only window with that view.

She saw Jiggs first. He was striding way out in front, looking happy to be loose—his nose lifted, searching. Her father followed, carrying a plastic bucket by the rim, its handle long gone.

He wasn't a dozen yards past the barn when he stopped. He whistled for Jiggs, and then bent over and dumped the mice onto the grass. He whistled again and started back. He picked a piece of straw from the bucket and let it fall.

Even in the near dark, Mary saw that it was the same quick gulp Jiggs had used before. She pinched her eyes shut, everything black. She heard a voice in her head. She had to open her eyes right away and look again. *What's this?* the voice said. *What's this?*

Her father walked toward the barn and tapped out the bucket. Nothing was left.

Papermaker Pride

WE WERE THE Kemper Papermakers, and we had Papermaker pride. Our mascot was the paper wasp, the school's colors red and white. We put a K on the wasp's chest, a bowler hat on his head, and logging boots on his feet. In some pictures he carried a boom box with musical notes ascending from it, showing how we would fucking rock you.

Our school halls testified to our rockingness—case after display case of trophies, plaques, and other horseshit of that nature. The building reeked of athleticism, which smelled much like Drakkar Noir. On game days players wore their jerseys to school, and despite the other-day emphasis on name brands and designer labels, donning a jersey lifted you to the highest rank of social status. The soccer team was different, though, and the only time I ever wore my jersey to school was freshman year. Even in my red and white, I still got shoved against some lockers and called a retard.

The other teams bought new uniforms every couple seasons. Our jerseys were decades old and one hundred percent polyester, the collars stretching to our shoulders. The uniforms had been made way before baggy was in, and on all but the skinniest they fit like shrink-wrap. Our shorts were so short the whitest parts of our legs showed, and our competitors whistled at us.

The Papermaker soccer team got no pep rallies, no cheerleaders, no band. Many in the student body didn't even know Kemper had a soccer team. Besides Mandy, who was one of our fullbacks, girls didn't really come to our games, unless they were friends of Mandy's, and they were all dogs anyway. Because the football coach didn't want us to tear up his turf, the soccer team played on the middle school's field, which was across from the paper mill. The mill took up five or six blocks along the river downtown and it never stopped running. Trains hauled in endless loads of poplar, which was stacked in big piles near the boarded-up Kmart.

In the north corner of the soccer park, Kemper's water tower loomed over us, as tall as the mill's smokestacks. On clear days the smoke and steam rose from the mill in long, trailing clouds all the way down the valley, and on cloudy, socked-in days, Kemper reeked of rotten egg. Our field was never watered, and in the fall the grass browned and turned to dust. The set of pingy, aluminum bleachers had a trash can chained to it. An old, cinder-rock track surrounded the playing field, and Coach West had us run two laps on that track before every practice, the drum of our cleats like the paper presses—rhythmic, dull.

Coach West's main qualification as our soccer coach was that he was English. No one had ever seen him actually play soccer. He hardly even touched the ball during practice. If one rolled over to him, he'd send a pointy kick back at us—often off-target, so we'd have to chase it down. Practices consisted of running the two laps and then scrimmaging for forty-five minutes. Coach West had been using the format for years, and he used it again during my time on the team. Start of senior year, my high school record stood at two and nineteen.

By day, Coach West sold windows, and he came to every game and practice wearing the clothes from his real job. On colder days, he'd wear an insulated, vinyl jacket with *Pella* silk-screened on its back. Otherwise it was just a pair of dress shoes, dress slacks, and a shirt with a normal-sized collar. He'd lost much of his accent, but his voice still sounded rough and foreign enough that I guess we sometimes believed he knew what he was talking about, even when he was talking about winning.

The most ridiculous, maddening ritual of practice was when Coach West would get pissed about where someone was standing on the field. We were supposed to be constantly setting up triangles, weaving the ball up or downfield, just one-two-three around the other team. But we didn't have that game. Blow all if we could actually make the ball go where we wanted it to go. Our game was more of a kick-it-and-hope type, one where we'd mostly just kick the ball as hard as we could, as far as we could, and then run after it.

"Where I'm pointing," Coach would scream, sweeping his arm, indicating the entire mid-field. He'd use a sucked-on toothpick to lengthen his aim. "Stand there!" he'd yell. "Can't you see where I'm pointing?"

Often we were already standing exactly where Coach West was pointing while he was yammering at us about standing where he was pointing. It confused a lot of the younger kids who didn't realize you just had to go stand somewhere else, even if it wasn't where he was pointing, and then he would shut up.

❧

SENIOR YEAR I was one of three captains: me and Raymaker and our goalie, Kobbs. Our team had plenty of other idiots, too. The three freshmen were skinny and bird-boned, feathers to push around. Putman was the best of them, always smirking, and every time he faked me out in practice I'd trip him from behind. Van Grinsven, a junior, had Ectodermal Dysplasia, which, in his case, basically meant he didn't have sweat glands. His skin tone was like a pastel version of mop water, and he didn't have much hair on his head, none at all on the rest of his body. He kept a spray bottle of water on the sidelines, plus towels to soak and drape over himself. His condition, his life in the hell that was Kemper High, left him with a lot of issues to work out, and no matter how bad we were getting beaten you could count on him to keep tackling cleat-first.

We had Kobbs's little brother, Kenny, who supposedly ate out a chick while she was on the rag. We had Milner, who did things in study hall like pull out his balls or see how long he could hold his lighter under his arm, to the point of gnarly burns. Gus, that year's foreign exchange student, our Swedish surprise, was the only way we ever had half a chance.

We liked Gus, and Raymaker and I made an effort to show him around a little. The night after our first game we took him to Butch's Pizza. My mom and my stepfather, Mike, had given me a used full-size Dodge van on my sixteenth, and if I was back by curfew, and it was just Raymaker I was hanging with, I could use it whenever. Raymaker called it the Party Barge.

"Great game," Raymaker said, grabbing Gus by the shoulders after he got in. Gus had scored Kemper's first goal in almost a year, and though we were already down five points when it happened, we nearly got a delay of game for how long we celebrated. "We're totally going to get you laid tonight," Raymaker said. We totally had no way of doing that.

Gus was somewhat baby-faced for a Viking, and he smelled a bit like snot, and the only people he hung out with were the band geeks. His voice was high-pitched, especially when he was excited. "American girls," he said, chirping like a finch.

"Kemper girls," Raymaker said. "Milk fed."

Butch's was nearly empty, and we sat next to a window that had a red and white paper wasp painted on it. After football games the whole restaurant filled, but we were one night early. It was the only place to go in Kemper that wasn't a bar or supper club, and Butch was the actual guy who made the pizzas. Gus had never seen one served cut into squares. "The best ones are these," I said, grabbing the tiniest, crispiest pieces along the edges.

Across the street sat the Kmart, and as we hung in the booth looking at the empty pizza tin, a train rumbled out of town, the horn signaling each crossing. Gus's host family had given him money for the whole meal, and for a long time we played with the change, flicking the pennies across the table and down the aisle. We'd already put our jackets on to leave when Coach West came in for carryout. He walked straight over.

"I hope these guys aren't getting you into trouble," he said to Gus.

"Moderate," Raymaker said.

"No trouble," Gus said, "just fun."

Coach West looked happy. A pack of cigarettes bulged his shirt pocket, and his eyes were loose and glossy. "Nice work out there tonight," he said. "All three of you." I thought he was the kind of guy who never actually listened to what he was saying. "I think we'll do all right this year. I've got a good feeling." Good feeling was something he said at the start of every season. He'd already said it after the game.

Butch brought Coach's pizza over to the cash register, and Coach West pointed his checkbook at us.

I pointed back. "Order up."

"Let's be ready to practice tomorrow," he said, all inspirational. "One hundred percent. One hundred and a half."

I drove us around the back of Butch's after we left, over to the used car lot where the Party Barge had come from. It was a small place that didn't keep the lot lit up at night. Bright helium-filled balloons swayed at the ends of their tethers, each tied to a vehicle's antenna.

"Have you heard of cow tipping?" I asked Gus. "Well this is kind of like that," I said, "but not."

The night was cast orange from the lights at the mill, and we sat on top of the Party Barge and watched the balloons. We'd untied every single one, and if you kept focused on them, it almost felt as if you too were lifting away. As if luck came as easily as boredom. The balloons drifted toward the river and kept floating higher, until they disappeared in the stars.

"Can you still see them?" I asked.

Gus kept saying, "Yeah, man."

A couple weeks before Homecoming, Coach West gathered us up on the bleachers. "We'll run our laps in a minute," he said. "Listen up."

The first point of order was a Homecoming announcement: the Homecoming committee had decided to try something stupid. Each sports team was to select a representative to sit on the Homecoming court. "Our team is in a little different situation," Coach West said. "We're going to have two." Mandy, of course, would be one. "And so then what we need to do is vote on who goes with her."

"We have to be Mandy's date?" Raymaker asked, his voice rising like Gus's.

"All right!" Kenny shouted.

"This isn't a date," Coach West said.

It was obvious that Gus should be our representative, and I said as much. He had been scoring goals all season and had brought us within a point of actually winning a game. "Plus," I said, "this is like the ultimate American experience for him."

"Mandy!" Kobbs yelled, shaking Gus by the neck, everyone except Mandy laughing. Even Coach West chuckled.

"Talk about it," Coach West said, coming back around to the serious business that was soccer, "and then you guys can decide after practice." He stood in front of us rubbing his palms together, as if to warm them. "One more thing," he added. The athletic director had asked him to resign at the end of the season, and Coach had agreed. "This will be it for me."

MIKE AND MY mom had me stand in front of the fireplace for the pictures. At first they'd wanted to capture it all on the front lawn, but I finally talked them into sparing me.

"You'd look so nice in your sport coat," my mom said. She flipped on another light. "Are you sure you don't want to wear it?"

"He looks sharp," Mike said, like a real chum.

Raymaker had convinced everyone to vote for me. "How many pictures do you need?" I asked.

"Be proud of this," my mom said, and pinched me on the elbow.

The parade started from the municipal building, and all the Homecoming representatives were supposed to be there fifteen minutes early. Before I could leave home, my mom had to re-pin my boutonniere. She kept trying to mess with my hair. I had gone as far as contemplating a scenario in which I had asked a girl to the dance, but no further. Mike gave me a big handshake with a twenty-dollar bill hidden in his palm. "Remember to sit up straight," he said. "Come on, don't roll your eyes."

When I got to the staging area, the band was already warming up. Fire trucks idled, their siren lights flashing. The floats were lined up by class, freshman first. We were playing the Rockets that year, and the senior float had a Papermaker football player straddling a very boner-esque rocket. Behind the floats, Kemper's veterans—some old guys from the old wars, a couple of kids from the new—waited in their convertibles, each with a hand-painted Papermaker sign trailing from the back bumper. Mr. Skarpinski, the vice principal, had gathered up some of the Homecoming representatives and was waving me over.

"Everybody all set?" he asked. He had a bullhorn tucked under one of his armpits.

Melissa Burns, cheerleading selectee, was passing out bags of candy. Mandy and the girls' cross-country star, Shelly Van Zeeland, were missing.

"Be careful when you're throwing these," Mr. Skarpinski said. "And not all at once. You'll go from here, along Main Street, and then over to the high school. Just wave, smile, have fun."

"Can I have some of this?" Craig Schumacher asked. He'd pretty much busted like a thousand touchdowns that season. He started chewing on one of the bags.

"Sure," Mr. Skarpinski said, looking at his watch. "A little."

Everyone giggled, as if this wasn't about to be the most horrible moment of our lives. Mr. Skarpinski spread his arms and started urging us toward the cars.

"Mandy isn't here," I said, praying.

"Band," Mr. Skarpinski said. The parade counted as credit for her final grade, so she was marching with the band.

"I'm not riding with Mandy?" I asked, spinning around so that I was walking backwards, facing Mr. Skarpinski, who was shaking his head no.

Gus had talked Coach West into making the team run portions of our laps backwards as a way to improve agility. Every time Gus said *switch*, the team would clap and turn, one of us usually wiping out. I was doing the Homecoming Shuffle, and I clapped my hands and spun back, stepping on one of Craig Schumacher's heels.

"Shelly is also in band," Mr. Skarpinski added. "You'll be sharing a car with Andy."

Andy Meyers overheard Mr. Skarpinski and nodded at me. We were in Algebra II together, and he raised his hand much more often than I did. Andy was thin as newspaper, and because he could outrun everyone and could go for miles, he seemed to get treated pretty fairly. "We've got that badass black one," he said, pointing to a streak-free Mustang.

Our driver, white-haired and liver-spotted, wore a VFW ball cap and asked us to take off our shoes so we wouldn't rub any dirt into the backseat. We were the last in the string of representatives. I was happy Mandy was wetting her reed. A long V of geese cut across the sky, and Andy and I twisted our heads to look, the bags of candy sitting in our laps.

As we moved down our route, more and more people lined Main Street. Families brought hot chocolate, red-and-white blankets, miniature pompoms. Little kids waved like they wanted to shake free of their own arms. Workers crowded the fire escapes at the mill, and the drumbeats echoed off the buildings. I didn't see Coach West anywhere. When we passed my mom and Mike, Mom blew kisses at me while Mike mouthed for me to correct my posture. Each time the fire trucks hit the air horns, I flinched, my eyes welling.

"This is kind of cool," I said, leaning over to Andy. He was smiling at an elderly couple sitting in a pair of lawn chairs. "I thought it was going to suck."

All the seniors had gotten together at Oak Street, where the parade turned off Main and headed for the high school. Girlfriends wore boyfriends' jerseys. A few guys painted their faces. Craig Schumacher had saved a bag of candy, and he threw the whole, unopened thing at his buddies. He stood up in the back of the convertible and started posing like he'd scored a touchdown, everyone eating it up, until Melissa grabbed him by the seat of his pants and pulled him back down. I spotted Raymaker and Gus, both laughing at me, and I tried flashing them a secret, quick bird.

"Go 'Makers!" Raymaker screamed.

It was then, noticing Raymaker crying at the top of his lungs, as if another ball had hit the back of our net and he was yelling at us to never give up, imploring us to reach down to some level of ourselves where our wills hadn't been broken, that I clearly sensed the doom ahead, though it should have been obvious all along.

"Look at the cute couple," someone shouted at Andy and me.

It continued. "What up, boyfriends?"

"Check out the fag float."

"The king and the king."

Andy and I glanced briefly at each other, and I wondered, though I've never come to know, if he was thinking that it was my fault, because I was thinking the same about him. His fault. Raymaker's fault. Mandy's fault. Probably mine, too. Up ahead the procession had bunched, and our driver slowed to a near stop. I tried laughing along, but then I felt my face go slack, felt it turn as hot as August blacktop, and the sounds—the band playing "Louie Louie" for the second time, the fire trucks, the crowd— they all faded away.

Somehow, Oak Street was lined with maples, and red leaves dropped with the breeze like some horrible, heavy snow. The classmates who were not ruining my life picked up piles and threw them at each other. I turned and waved to a little girl on the other side of the street, but she wasn't even looking—she was just learning to walk.

"Up the butt!" people chanted, halting on each word. Up. The. Butt.

ॐ

During halftime, the Homecoming representatives were called out to the football field and coupled up. Andy and I made sure to stand far apart. Craig Schumacher stood arm in arm with Melissa Burns, whose knees looked blue from the cold. The game had been a low-scoring, defensive struggle, and Kemper was only up by a field goal. Steam curled off Craig in waves, his jersey streaked with mud and bones.

The announcer named each of us, plus the sport we represented. Mandy was wearing her band uniform. Her blazer fit tight around the midsection and was buttoned up for the weather. She kept pulling at the fingertips of her white gloves.

"I'll see you at the dance?" she asked. I was sure she'd heard how the parade had gone, was sure everyone had, and I was waiting for an apology.

"I don't know," I said, "I'm not positive I'm going."

"Really?" she asked, looking at me, for some insane reason, like mine was the dumb idea.

Above us in the crowd, our fellow students were being spastic, stomping on the bleachers and being bodysurfed by a shirtless Dan Derks, who'd been kicked off the football team earlier in the year for drinking.

"It's something to do," I admitted.

"I think I have issues," Mandy said to me, "with your thought process."

To loud applause, Craig and Melissa were announced King and Queen. Craig lifted Melissa from under the armpits, twirled her in a circle, and kissed her when he set her back down. Then he ran across the field toward the locker room, pumping his helmet into the sky as he went.

ॐ

For most of the night, Raymaker and I sat backwards in the lunchroom chairs and watched the dance floor from a dark corner. We were pretty sure that at any second the hottest girls in school were going to come throw themselves at us, so we didn't really make the effort. Gus had asked Kimmy Wurdinger, his host sister's best friend, to the dance. They spent a lot of the night together, and not just during the slow songs. The DJ was the same lame guy who'd done like every dance we'd ever had, so we knew to stay upwind of his smoke machine. When he played a good song, something hard, Raymaker and I drummed the air.

We weren't the only ones. All around the room, pushed back to the walls, out of the strobe lights' range, clusters of non-dancers had formed. Van Grinsven parked himself in front of a stack of chairs, and any time anyone came to grab one his expression seemed to say both *Die!* and *Please be my friend!*

Putman was standing next to his date, who was talking to some other girl. He had his hands in his pockets, and nodded at everyone, and I could see from the lines on his forehead that he was trying hard not to blow his chances. Over by the hallway doors, Mandy had circled together with some of her friends. Jesse Derks, her acned knight, stretched an arm around her waist, and the two of them sat there with straight backs and stupid smiles, Mandy tapping her toes to the music.

"You want her," Raymaker said, chucking me on the shoulder, noticing how I'd been watching her.

"Why?" I asked.

"Nature."

"I'm going to have to dance," I said, thinking about how awkward it was at practice when one of us got partnered doing groin stretches with her. "As a couple."

After Craig and Melissa were crowned, the Homecoming court, holding our arms up as if they were swords, formed an aisle to the dance floor. After our King and Queen swayed together in the center of the room for half a song, the DJ cut in, inviting the runners-up and the rest of the court to join. With my hands flat against Mandy's hips, with her hands on my shoulders, and space between us, we shifted from side to side, slowly turning in a circle.

"Are you having a good time?" she asked.

"I don't know," I said. "It can't get worse."

I was a foot taller than Mandy, and though I wished I could stop, I kept breathing in the sweet perfume of her hair. She was easy to steal the ball from, and she got knocked over hard at least once a scrimmage. Why she didn't quit, why she didn't play a sport at Kemper that had a girl's team—who knew?

"I voted for Van Grinsven," she finally said.

When the DJ opened the floor, couples poured in. Kimmy Wurdinger even grabbed Raymaker and pulled him out. "It's fine if you want to quit," Mandy said to me, shrugging her shoulders, "I'd like to dance with Jesse."

"It's okay," I said. I squeezed her hands tighter. "Let's finish this song."

❧

MIDWAY THROUGH THE last game of the season, the score was already twelve-zero. Even beating us so badly, Menasha kept their starters in after halftime. Just as the ref was putting his whistle to his mouth to start the half, Coach West ran out onto the field waving his arms and stopping the kickoff. This was the final forty-five minutes of his career. It was our possession, and Coach West came over to the center circle, holding a hand up to the official. "Give me a minute," he said, moving toward Menasha's bench.

I stood next to Gus, whose magic foot was on the ball. "We forfeit?" he asked.

Coach West was talking with Menasha's coach, pointing to the kids on the bench.

"You have to do that before you even start," I said.

"We haven't started," Gus argued.

"Before you even start the *game*."

Coach West slowly shook his head side to side, much like Gus was doing. Coach stuffed his hands in his jacket pockets and walked back across the field, yelling at Raymaker who was sitting cross-legged on the ground. I looked to Coach for some indication of what to do, but he just stood there looking back at us, as if he had nothing left, which was likely.

"Gentlemen," the referee said.

I told Gus to pass it to me.

On the whistle I took the ball and went straight at them. Menasha hadn't needed to do much all game, because eventually we kicked the ball right into their feet. Once we'd even kicked it into our own goal. But while Gus had been talking about a forfeit, I'd had enough. I ran past one Menasha player, then a second, a third. When I'd made it through the midfielders, suddenly everyone started to wake up—the players, the parents, Coach West. I kicked the ball past the sweeper and ran shoulder to shoulder with him, trying to chase down my chance. On the sidelines, Van Grinsven's mom started screaming, the pitch and emotion rising with each exclamation—*Go! Go! Go!* Even I started to believe I was going to make it.

I stuck out my right arm to block the defender and moved the ball ahead. The goalie and I met eyes, and he watched me look one way, then the other. He came forward trying to close his angle, and I planted my left foot, swung back and took a shot, a hard fast one right into his hands.

A collective Papermaker sigh drifted across the field. Van Grinsven's mom practically wailed. Menasha played on, even as all the rest of us stood frozen. Van Grinsven's mom did the only thing she knew how to do. She gathered herself and yelled for us to run.

Coach West's hands had come out of his pockets. "That's it," he said, back in the fight. He shuffled along the sideline and pointed toward our goal. "Back!" he screamed. "Get back!"

At fifteen-zero, Menasha's starters stayed in the game. At sixteen. Seventeen. Our faces were blotchy from the chilly air. Any time play slowed, we stood around with our hands on top of our heads. When Menasha put the eighteenth point into the back of our net, Coach West came onto the field, and before Kobbs could kick the ball back up to center, Coach West took it from him. Coach started walking toward the referee, who was blowing his whistle and waving his arms in the air. I knew—from our football, basketball, and baseball squads—that to win a state championship a team had to be killers, so I didn't hold it against Menasha. But then Coach did something we'd never seen him do. When the referee reached for the ball, Coach West pulled it back and then turned and punted it for the street.

The first kick went straight up. After two more tries, Coach West finally wrestled the ball from a parent and threw it into the road, where it rolled toward the mill's entrance gate. The referee had been holding up his red card and tooting his whistle through the whole scene. Coach

West wasn't even allowed to stay on the field. He watched the rest of the game from his car.

❧

WE LOST TWENTY to nothing, which was a record for both teams. Kobbs told us not to shake hands with Menasha after the game, and when they realized we weren't coming out to centerfield, Menasha huddled up and started a call-and-response, shouting, "Mash!" then, "*Ya!*" while beating on their chests. Even in the cold, a few of them took off their shirts so we'd be sure to see how big their muscles were.

I sat on the bench next to Raymaker with my socks pulled down, my shin guards unfastened and pushed out. My mom and Mike had come down out of the bleachers and were waving goodbye to me. Mike had the same camera he'd taken the Homecoming pictures with hanging from his neck, and my mom, I could tell, wanted to pull me close and say something soothing, as was her way. I was looking through them, pretending they weren't there, looking toward what I hoped was a future unplagued by the same problems my team had with talent. Across the street, the workers on the fire escape flicked their cigarettes into the parking lot and went back inside.

"Butch's?" Raymaker asked. What else was there?

We found Coach West leaning against the Party Barge. With the palm of his hand, he patted the passenger side panel. "Lads," he said, trying to sound upbeat.

Gus and Raymaker and I stood and waited for something more. Coach seemed to be thinking.

"We tried," Gus said, elbowing Raymaker off the curb.

"If I embarrassed you," Coach West said, reaching to shake our hands. It wasn't just him. It was everything.

"Coach," I said, freeing my hand. I assured him it was all right. "It was cool," I said, dreaming that I knew a thing or two about what cool was.

"I just really wanted to win," he growled.

Same as us all.

The Lumberjack's Story

I WAS TURNING my undershirt inside-out and getting ready for bed when Jenkins come over and started in on a story he'd told me a hundred times before. The story was about a belly-robber named Garland who'd throw raisins into the pies whenever we had a fly problem in camp.

A cold draft blew through the chinks in the logs, and no matter how much moss we stuffed in those gaps, a little snow still found its way inside. This late at night there wasn't much fun left in sitting around and smoking. The lice would take until morning to crawl back to the inside of my shirt, but Jenkins had already built himself a head of steam.

This Norwegian we called Bigs finally chased Garland out of camp. Bigs took a fishing pole and went damn full after him. After that, our head cook was a feller named Harvey, and he treated us pretty decent, and we never starved.

Bigs was a tough son of a bitch whose real name was Guttorm. We called him Bigs because he was the biggest man in camp. Most camps, the cook was king, but in ours it was Bigs. It was Bigs, then Harvey, then George Stickney, the company boss.

Most at the camp wore beards, but some of us really was just boys and the hair on our faces was thin and patchy. It was my first season away from home. Bigs had thick, black hair—bear fur. One of his eyes was dead and milky and always seemed to be looking straight ahead. He wore an old beehive hat, and if that hat was on the deacon seat, and one of us wanted to sit in that spot, well we didn't dare move it.

After Jenkins went on for a little while, I realized he was only talking about Garland to tell me about something else. When Garland was run out, I'd seen it myself, so I didn't need someone telling me about it all over again. I put my arm around Jenkins's shoulder and started walking him toward the pig stove, which a few men was still circled around. The others slept. We were tired at night, even if it was twenty stinking men in one long bed.

"Someone tried to chase me out," Jenkins said, "I don't know that I'd mind."

I said, "Tell me in the morning."

Before Garland, it was this German feller that Bigs had chased off. The German tried one quick punch before he was knocked cold. I'd heard Bigs had busted quite a few men over the years, and that it took a special man, a real special fool, to partner up with Bigs for a season. Jack Whittin was our current fool.

Whittin wore a little curl at the end of his mustache and was the fanciest man in camp. His clothes come from Montreal, and they was always in good shape. Though we didn't say it, if a feller had too many patches and sewed-up spots on his clothes, well then we thought maybe he wasn't quite the lumberjack he said he was.

We all liked a sharp ax. Some nights in camp Bigs would join Whittin, and they'd stand at the two wheels, pumping the foot pedals hard, running stone against metal and putting an edge to it. When Bigs got his ax nice and sharp, he'd usually give it a good throw and stick it in the wall. It was early March, and we'd been in the woods a long time, and everyone was sore with everyone in one way or another.

"You thinking about fishing?" I asked Jenkins. "Or pondering something else?"

I'd thought about quitting myself, many times, but I'd always stopped short. If I was Whittin, I would've been broken months ago. I'd gotten along by telling myself that it was impossible to leave, that there was nowhere to go, and after a while, when I started believing it, I felt fairly right about everything, however flea-bitten and rough.

"Could be both," Jenkins said to me. "A little, anyway."

Our boots hung from the drying racks near the stove. The heat was fading, and I slid mine and Jenkins's pair closer. None of us had taken baths since the first deep snow. The bunkhouse smelled awful, of those boots and sweat and tobacco and beans, and sometimes in the night the smell was suffocating.

"Good night, Jenkins," I said, patting him on the stomach, leaving him near a bucket of ashes.

THE BEST WAY of taking the mornings was to just get working. Old Stamper, our teamster, he woke up right after Harvey, while we still got a little sleep. The first thing Stamper did each morning was go out barefoot to the stables and feed his oxen. He'd come back a short time later and sit on the bench and carefully brush off his pink feet before he put on his socks and boots. The old man swore it gave him warm toes all day.

Even with a belly full of sweet pads and tea, I was cold every morning, so I just pulled my hat as low as I could for the ride out, and I kept my head down and tried to think about how still and quiet the forest was, or how dumb, yet strong, them oxen seemed. If I thought about being warm, or the smell of a girl, or some easy idea that I'd had the night before, the morning would be miserable. Except for the commands by Old Stamper to his animals, we hardly talked on those rides out in the mornings. When we reached the line where we'd stopped the day before, Old Stamper would drop us off, and we'd get started again. Before anything else, we took off our mackinaws and hung them in the branches.

For most of the season, Jenkins and me was clean-up men, and we trimmed the branches off trees that guys like Whittin and Bigs felled. If there wasn't any dropped trees from the afternoon before, we'd start the day helping the choppers clear spaces around the trees they was about to cut. Toward the end of the season, Jenkins and me worked as sawyers, and we bucked the trees into sections. Some were sawyers the whole season, but me and Jenkins was only at it for a few weeks before the drives.

Jenkins had a bad way of riding the saw, which mostly came by way of his always wanting to talk about something. It was hard to talk and saw at the same time. We were clearing the forest bare, and in between the thunder of them falling trees, we usually made less noise than the songbirds. Most times the fellers communicated with grunts, often in completely different languages—*Nej! Non!*—but Jenkins unwound these long, meandering sermons about men who'd set their bottles of whiskey next to bottles of carbonic and forgot which was which in the middle of the night, or of arsonists who'd gone and set fire to the asylums they'd been removed to, stories that Jenkins seemed to think had a sense of justice in them, but not hardly a point.

Sometimes he got lost and forgot where the story was going, or he'd finish one and not know where to start the next, and then the saw would start returning slower and slower. He'd be looking out into the woods, letting me do all the work, which I sometimes did, because I thought it made me the stronger man.

"Tell me a real tall one," I'd say.

Sometimes I'd stop the saw, right as we switched directions, I'd stop the saw so Jenkins would slip, until one time he fell and cut himself bad, and I never did that again.

Sometimes I'd curse his name.

"No one misses him," I said about Garland the morning after I'd left Jenkins by the pig stove. We was working on the side of a rise near the river. "His potatoes tasted like pinecones," I said.

Jenkins didn't say anything. The clouds was low and gray, and it was damp and warm, and as the morning went on, clumps of snow fell from the trees. I watched Jenkins sniff the air. His nose was crooked from a bad spill he'd taken on the drive last spring. The air smelled of the hemlock we'd just sawed.

We moved down the tree to make another cut. I knew Jenkins was trying to get back at me a little, and now that I wanted him to talk, he wouldn't. I knew it because he wasn't dragging, and no matter how many times I tried looking him in the eyes, Jenkins stayed on the cutting and kept his mouth shut. We went on like that until I couldn't take it no more.

"It's awful risky," I said. "But we could steal some of Harvey's bread dough, and take some hooks, and then go bust a hole in the ice. I know we'd catch a few."

After a minute, he finally let on and smirked. "We'd have to come back with a big one," he said.

"A fish to feed the camp."

WE WAS PLAYING hot-ass one Saturday night and Whittin was it. With his hat covering his face, Whittin was bent over in front of everybody and we was taking turns whacking him on the rear. The air inside was smoked up, and the fiddler was playing songs I didn't know the names of, from countries I'd never been to, and we had us a pretty good game going—meaning Whittin was getting furious.

When someone smacked him, Whittin yelped and jumped a little, standing and twisting his hat as if that would wring the sting from his butt.

"It was you," Whittin said to the wrong person. His face was red as a blister. "I know it was you!"

We grabbed our hats and slapped them in our hands, or against our legs, or we threw them on the ground, beating them soft. A feller could be a good sport about hot-ass for a little while, but if he couldn't guess who'd hit him the first couple tries, it was easy to get cross, and once he got cross that's when everyone really started having fun. If a feller was mad about it, the laughing only made him hotter, and he could hardly think of a name to shout. There was a pecking order in a logging camp, and we spent a lot of time on it, and though there was plenty of work to do in the woods, it seemed to be our one true constant task.

Right then, Whittin was on the very bottom.

All of us knew Whittin had been stretched—Bigs had whetted him down all winter—so we was all that much rougher on him. We was lumberjacks, and when we saw something ready to drop, we had to put our hands on it and push it over.

"Again!" we shouted. We stomped along with the music and sang. "Again!"

I decided to take a shot at him. I danced around Whittin a little first. Wide stripes of sweat run down his back. When I hollered, he flinched. The fiddler was racing, and someone had picked up the accordion, someone the mouth harp. The jug was going around, not to drink, but to play.

"It's gonna sting!" Jenkins yelled.

As I went to hit, a hand grabbed my arm and spun me around. Bigs's milky eye looked down at me, just like his good one. For a second I thought he might knock me out. In that second, all those reasons I'd had for leaving camp early come back, and I started asking myself why I hadn't just sucked up the shame of it and left. In front of us, Whittin was quivering.

When he let go of my hand, Bigs started walking circles around Whittin. After a few turns, Bigs motioned for me to follow. Bigs shook the floor with each footstep, and I pretended to stomp like it was me shaking the ground. I thought about goosing Whittin first, before Bigs, because I thought it'd somehow one-up him. It was something we all wanted to do, but never chanced.

After he quit circling, I started backing away, but then Bigs stopped me and leaned close.

"As hard as you can," he whispered.

The fiddler had built the song to a fire. It was a low-down thing to do, but for some reason we done lots of those low-down things, whether we meant to or not. Bigs had arms as long as pike poles, and his hands was big as paddles. He nodded, and we both swung.

Bigs stopped an inch short.

I hit Whittin with everything. He took off like a whipped horse, and when he went to catch himself he was too busy wringing his hat and cursing, and he fell down. If Bigs had joined in, we would have split him in half. Whittin slipped a little as he tried to get up, and then we laughed him right back into the ground. When Whittin saw that it was Bigs, he got up slow and graceful. Even though I was standing next to Bigs, I don't think Whittin had any idea about me. We was still all busting up.

"Goddamn the bunch of you!" Whittin screamed. "The goddamn whole bunch!"

The band had stopped, and the room was quiet, except for a few scuffling feet. I could hear someone chewing on a pipe stem.

"Get 'em, Whittin!" someone shouted.

Whittin stood there and straightened out his clothes some and put his hat back on his head. He took a look at himself and dusted off his vest a little more. He flipped the rim of his hat up, like he wore it out in the woods. Whittin pointed straight at Bigs, and then started toward him.

A few others backed me up. "No," I said to Whittin, putting my hand on his chest to slow him down. "*Non!*" I said. An elbow knocked me in the lip. Whittin's eyes was focused, hateful. "It wasn't him," I said, squashed between the two of them. Part of me wanted to let Whittin tear at Bigs, though I knew that wouldn't be no favor. Our Saturday night was over.

⁊

Because it was Sunday, we didn't go out in the woods. Instead we laid around camp and played cribbage, or boiled our clothes, or practiced with our axes. Each time Jenkins tried speaking to me, I told him I didn't want to talk about it. I knew I was a kid, and that I probably thought I was tougher than I really was, because I felt pretty miserable and sore that morning. Fresh socks was the best I could do for myself.

Even on Sundays, Old Stamper woke right after the cooks and went out to the stables. We could sleep in, but sleeping too long meant missing breakfast, and no one ever missed a meal unless he was sick. When Stamper come back in, he told Harvey that he'd found Whittin sleeping in the hay. Stamper asked Whittin if he'd done the feeding, and Whittin run off.

During the scuffle, Whittin had the same look I'd seen in others, in men who were convinced on doing something good reason said not to. I'd seen the same look on a feller who'd gotten real rough with a girl at a brothel down by Shawano, and when some guys tried to quiet him, he stabbed one of them with a little knife. I wanted to mark my spot among these men, but what I was feeling that morning was how my true mark was against the forest, and that the forest was dark and hard and unending. Whenever I tried to measure myself against it, I reached the same conclusion—I'd always be the smaller of the two.

My family, we had a little homestead going, but that was a two-day walk away. And my father, he'd nearly given up on the place, as he'd done with most things. Some of the others didn't even have that much, but some of them, I guess the ones who did have something, well they had themselves families and a little piece of cleared land and maybe some animals to fatten. But even them, they didn't have much, because we didn't have many other ways to earn a wage.

Whittin stayed away the rest of the day. Old Stamper went out late to the stables and looked, but Whittin was still gone. Some wolves cried real loud that night, and I knew we was all wondering if it was Whittin they'd gotten to.

Old Stamper had news the next morning. "He's out there," he said. "Whittin is back."

When we walked outside that day, Whittin was sitting on the sled and looking up into the pinery. If someone had a thing with another feller, and it had gotten bad, and the first feller didn't want it to get worse, he just kept quiet, and Whittin was keeping quiet.

We loaded up our peavies and saws and axes, and Old Stamper called to his oxen while a guy named Phillips started whistling a tune that began, *"What did you pay for them calfskin boots…"*

❧

SOME NIGHTS THE men would just make each other tell stories. If you wouldn't tell one, then you had to put some tobacco in the poor box, which anyone could take from, or maybe you had to do a little song and dance to get out of it. But mostly everyone just chose a story, because the way a feller told a story marked him, just like his clothes did, and no man liked to give up his tobacco, and none of us wanted to be dancing the quadrille alone in front of everybody else.

Some of the fellers chose to sit and tell their stories, while some of the others stood, sometimes pulling another feller into it, and sometimes— if the story was about a lady—dipping a feller and giving him a little kiss just to get a laugh. Some of the fellers had points to make, so they pounded fists to palms and raised their voices and spoke of moments that had come too late, always lamenting for us to listen. The better ones, the fellers who could tell the best stories, they spit into a bucket before they spoke, or they whittled on a piece, or they walked slow and quiet across the planks, in some manner that was like the ringing of a bell.

Now and then, when the roads weren't too bad, a peddler would come through selling suits. They was usually pretty good suits—guaranteed and measured to fit. He was always a pretty comical feller, and he'd tell us a few stories to entertain us before his pitch. Sometimes it was watches he was peddling, but that's how he always done it—some fabulous stories about knights and maidens, or crooked rivers pulled straight, and then the sale. If a feller told a real wild story, he was sure to sell something. Some of them peddlers probably would've made pretty good preachers, better than the few who dared come through, because these peddlers, when they spun something, they made us believe it was true, even though we knew it wasn't. Men gave away money they didn't even have.

≈

WHITTIN AND BIGS didn't tear each other apart, not like I thought they would. Instead they went and cut more trees in one day than anyone in this camp ever had. At the end of the day, when we all gathered at the tote road and waited for Stamper, Bigs stood at one end of the crowd, Whittin the other. We always worked until sundown, and the ride back to camp could be as cold as the ride out in the morning.

Where we'd cut, the sky was open and bright, but where we'd not worked, the trees blocked the sky. From under our hat brims, we watched Whittin and Bigs. Neither one of them said anything to anybody, and none of us said anything to them. Whittin stood still as could be. Bigs walked back and forth, kicking the snow like he was trying to get his toes warmed up. He wore a pair of heavy mittens, and he kept slapping his hands together so we would all know he was there. He and Whittin had sawed something incredible, and in his way Bigs was letting us know it was because of him—Bigs working Whittin into a rag. All of us could see, though, Whittin didn't look like no rag.

The next day the two of them cut even more trees, and it was the same thing while we waited for Stamper—Whittin standing calm, with clean mackinaw, mustache neat, and Bigs down the line, making some sort of bear noise. Bigs and Whittin was doing the work of two teams. The two of them started clearing smaller circles around the trees, because anytime a feller was clearing he wasn't chopping. One of the other teams had to pack up and move because Whittin and Bigs overrun them. The trees fell and fell and fell.

Whittin slept in the stables every night. He didn't say anything to any-body except Old Stamper. As the days passed, I started hiding under my brim less, and I paid more attention to Bigs, just as he was asking us to do. Outside, Bigs seemed as if he was always cold. His shoulders had rounded in, and his face grew paler even as the days got longer. Bigs began looking hollowed, like every partner he'd ever ruined. Bigs was trying to convince us that it was him who was setting the pace, but I could see he was actually trying to keep his hands and toes warm. He was trying to keep up.

Mostly, what Whittin said to Old Stamper was, "I'm going to kill him."

❧

BOSS STICKNEY SEEMED scared that Bigs would really go after Whittin, or Whittin after Bigs, and then Stickney's fine cutting machine would be dead. Whittin wasn't the first guy to say that he'd dust Bigs, but he was the first where we thought it might be true. Phillips even asked Bigs, "Is it true, Bigs?" Bigs went and slapped Phillips for that, which was supposed to mean no, but which we knew meant yes.

Sap started running that week, and Harvey tapped a few of the maples near camp. He'd boil that sap into syrup, even though we always had plenty to pour on everything. Pine pitch gummed up our saws and slowed us down, but if a feller had himself a little kerosene, he could take it off. Everyone who could find a bottle had some, but bottles was hard to come by, and they broke pretty easy.

Whittin carried some kerosene, and he'd clean his tools before he'd stop and eat. We ate our lunches and dinners out where we were working, and Harvey would make a big fire to sit around. We ate off tin plates, and the heat of the food warmed our hands. Even though we was out in the woods, that kerosene could stink up a feller's meal if he was downwind of it, but not one of us said anything about it to Whittin. Sometimes, the wind would shift, and a group of us would all get up at once to move. No one even dared say, "Heck, Whittin, you sure is cutting down a hell of a lot of trees." Rule was you ate in silence, and so we did.

The last lunch we ate with Whittin was no different from that. Whittin hung the piece of old shirttail he'd used to clean his saw on a branch, and then he took a plate. Far away, a ruffed grouse drummed. The wood in the fire was a little green, and it let out a steady hiss. When we was done with our grub, we gave our plates to the bull cook to wash, though we'd already licked them as clean as they needed to be.

After lunch the men split off, and that afternoon Jenkins and me was working a good ways from Bigs and Whittin. Instead of wiping our saws, we just poured the kerosene into the cut we was making. Jenkins started telling me about Mrs. Kuhlmann, who was not a woman, but a man, and I was thinking how I'd made it. Soon the rivers would be running. By the time a feller started worrying about pine pitch, he knew he was almost done.

Once the drive started, and the men went whatever way they was going to go—home, or downriver—talk about Bigs and Whittin would spread. It was the kind of thing men would be talking about for seasons, and I started thinking about that, how if I was working in some other part of the territory and someone brought the story up, I wanted to be able to say, "Yes, I sure was there." And if someone asked, "Well, how many trees was you taking?" I might say, "None, but I sure bucked plenty." And if they asked, "Plenty?" I wanted to be able to say something that made them quiet.

"Jenkins," I said, "I've had enough Mrs. Kuhlmann for now."

"There's more."

"None that I care to hear."

"A whole congregation," he said, after a second. "She had a whole congregation fooled."

I like to think it was sometime when I was straightening Jenkins out that Whittin set Bigs right. Pitch grabbed at our saw again, and another grouse was making a fuss. The sun felt warm, and after so many months of cold, it was making me dizzy.

Jenkins tried telling me one more thing about her, so I started pulling as fast and hard as I could. Jenkins was a son of a bitch, and I made him pay, though he matched my pace the whole time.

But Whittin had run Bigs thin out, and in the middle of another tree, Bigs just stopped cutting and set down on the soft ground. He rested his hands on his knees. When the fellers who was nearby seen what was happening, they passed it along. One by one, the teams set down their tools, or leaned against them.

Jenkins and me stopped racing each other and stood and listened and turned that way even though we had no chance of seeing. What I know of all this was sent down a line of men. Whittin stood and stared at Bigs, and Bigs sat looking at his own hands. We all stayed like that, catching our breath, for a good long while.

"Well," Whittin finally said, "the hell you will." He took hold of his end of the saw and waited.

What we'd all been expecting, it was about to happen, and that made me feel good, because there is a certain amount of comfort in being ready for something. Bigs stood and balled his fists and growled. He made it to Whittin in a few strides and tried to tackle him, but Whittin ducked out of the way.

Bigs slid on the snow and fell, and then Whittin jumped on him. He took him by the neck and shook. Bigs pounded on Whittin, right on the head, but Whittin wouldn't let go for nothing. Bigs stopped pounding and tried biting Whittin's hands, but they was clamped on Bigs's throat and he couldn't reach. Then he just started turning pink.

When Bigs passed out, Whittin let go.

❧

I WOKE UP the next morning before Harvey, and I laid on my back and stared into the dark and listened to all the men. I'd not slept much at all, because I'd tried listening for Bigs slipping out, or Whittin slipping in, but the only thing I'd heard all night was the strange whinny of a screech owl and the men breathing and sleeping and stinking. As I rested, scratching myself, I knew that when Old Stamper went out, Whittin wouldn't be there. It was not much different than dreaming about a pretty girl with soft hair who says kind things to you, and who lets you feel one of her pretty little breasts, and then waking up lonely, and knowing she wasn't ever there, though she seemed real.

"Gone," was all Old Stamper said when he come in and started dressing his feet.

Stickney partnered a guy named Eckly with Bigs. None of us volunteered, and Stickney didn't give Bigs the chance to choose. We could see the relief in Bigs by how his mouth was fit in his beard, which is to say it was hard to see, but it was there. And even though his shoulders was still rounded in, and he still looked cold, and his good eye was yellow and bloodshot, Bigs was smart enough to tell us how things stood again, and he sawed like a monster. Eckly couldn't even untie his boots that night.

How DOES A feller know if a lumberjack's story is good? Well, I liked stories that had a hero, though he's tough to find in some. After Whittin disappeared, Bigs tried reclaiming his throne, but it never was the same, and we did things to him that we never would've done before, like moving his hat, or picking fleas and setting them on his part of the bed. As often as not, he was the first feller asleep at night. Besides that day, each time Bigs and Eckly went out, they just did the same amount of work as the rest of us, sometimes less.

In the end, it hardly mattered for Bigs that Whittin walked away. We was on a slope up near Twenty Day, getting ready for the drive, breaking up the rollways. If a road had a hill that overlooked the river, instead of pushing them oxen that much farther all winter, Old Stamper would just pile the logs on the hillside to be dealt with in the spring.

We worked the rollways quiet, though we always told a feller what we was about to do before we did it. Mostly we listened to the logs, for once they started creaking and moaning, we knew they was about to bust loose. Often a whole hillside was caught up on just one or two stumps or saplings, and we had to find those pieces and unlock them. Once the logs was rolled into the river, they'd jam in the rapids below, where we'd set them free again.

Bigs didn't have a chance. A log above him swung free and hit him in the back. Then the whole pile started moving. When we finally got to Bigs, his head was smashed, and he'd been pushed face down into the ground, so that we had to undig him some before we could lift him. We set him on his back, and Stickney took off one of his own gloves and used it to wipe the mud from Bigs's face. The wet earth was pushed up into Bigs's mouth and nose, and it kept draining from them, and Stickney kept going back and clearing it away.

Bigs wasn't the only man to die that day. A half-breed named Dash Riechy went too, and we dug a grave for them under a big Norwegian pine because we figured that was about the best we could do. We put a stone at the head of each, in case their families wanted to come and find them, but none of us was certain if they had any. A lot of fellers was bruised and beat up by that accident, but not me, though that was only luck. We was men who could run down the length of a log while it was sliding downhill, and we ran until we had to jump, hoping we'd somehow fly clear of the whole mess.

Jenkins and I both went and finished the drive that year. It was a week down to Shawano, where the company stopped the night and most of us took to spending our wages in one way or another. I had a few bad swims, but I always made it to shore, or someone fished me out. You had to stand way back on a log to take it through a rapid, and you had to crouch low. I kept running down those logs and jumping off and hoping.

Downstream the river turned calm, and a lot of men wouldn't bother showing up for it in the morning. They was done. I walked to a little saloon at the end of town. It didn't have much except a counter to lean against and a couple lamps, and I drank a few drinks for Bigs and asked for rumors of Whittin. No one had heard of him, so I started telling them all about it.

On By

RITA RAN HER dogs in the fields across from our house. We saw her nearly every day, the long line of her sled team out front, the snow billowing behind. Some mornings Sara and I would stand together at the bay window, waiting for them. Neither of us had seen anything like it, and the dogs fascinated us. Until I met Rita at Borucki's, both Sara and I thought she'd be a man.

Borucki's held Elkton up. Mrs. Borucki pumped gas, shelved groceries, rented videos, kept live bait. A back corner of the store had been set aside as the town library. I was buying milk and pickles and a bag of salt for the walkway the night I met Rita. She was reading something inside the *Daily Journal*. Behind the neon signs in the window, the sky was black, heavy with night, hardly past five o'clock.

Mrs. Borucki slid my groceries across the counter and caught me staring at Rita. Mrs. Borucki had arms thin as craft dowels, freckled the whole length. A pencil slanted from the bun of her graying hair. "Brian," she said, "let me introduce you."

Rita wore an enormous blue parka that had an equally enormous hood. Her brown hair was pulled back into a thick braid. Her face was tan, but her hands pale, her fingernails dirty. She had soft, green eyes. One of her teeth sat sideways.

I'd just picked up the milk, and instead of setting it down, I used my left hand to shake with. From her grip, from her posture, I had a feeling that she split her own firewood.

"Well," I said, "stay warm."

Rita had parked in front of me. I'd left my car running. The one streetlamp in Elkton was directly above, and I couldn't see the stars for it. Rita's orange truck looked like it had once belonged to the highway department. A logo on the door had been painted over with primer, and rows of dog boxes now filled the truck's bed. Some of the dogs pressed their noses right up to the ventilation holes and whimpered at me. Steam panted into the sky. A piece of straw feathered down to the snow.

When I got home, Sara had already made dinner. The pickles were her dessert. It was anything pickled now: beet, carrot, cucumber, okra, onion—even egg at the tavern. Sara set a pot of chili in the center of the table. Our kitchen in Elkton was large enough for a table, and this was a first for us. We'd moved in just before the start of the school year, and what had seemed quaint and colorful, what had seemed new and fresh, now seemed drafty, and hard, and harshly lit.

"Do you like it?" Sara asked, about the chili, a string of yellow cheese dipping from lip to spoon. She had a figure almost as thin as Mrs. Borucki's, and she was wearing her sweatpants and sweatshirt, an outfit she rarely changed out of anymore.

"Did you use tomato juice?" I asked.

I needed the car to get to work, and all day Sara was stuck at home, surrounded by the snow. "It's what we had," she countered.

"I met her," I finally said later, after I'd finished my food. I was still sitting at our table, and Sara had moved in front of the TV. I knew she hated that I tried to have conversations with her when we weren't in the same room, but I didn't get up. "I met Rita," I said, louder. I, too, hated Sara trying to have conversations with me when we weren't in the same room.

"What's that?"

"Rita," I said.

Sara walked from the couch to the kitchen. She rested a hand on her hip. "I didn't hear a word of that."

"Her name is Rita."

Sara and I sat down to watch *A Bug's Life*, but were waiting for the weather forecast before pushing play. Sara thought the movie could be a good teaching tool for my kids at school. Sara was going to take notes for us, jot down our ideas during different scenes. She excelled at making lists: *snows, heavy, likely.*

"But I don't understand," she said. Sara couldn't believe that I hadn't asked Rita what kind of dogs they were, or how fast they could run, those things Sara and I wondered while watching her.

"We talked about the school."

"But I don't understand why you wouldn't ask."

"I don't know," I said. "I didn't think of it. She was on her way out the door."

BECAUSE OF THE storm front, school would be dismissed early. I left Sara's notes in my briefcase and handed out art supplies and told the kids to draw as many objects beginning with the letter R as they could. I stood at the window. Flakes of snow blew in every direction at once, gusts of wind howling and shaking the panes of glass. The clouds were bloated and gray, and it was so dark outside the automatic lights on the building's exterior stayed on. A rabbit had hopped across the playground and was now hiding underneath a hedge.

A kid could sit unaccompanied in Principal Donwood's office, as punishment, as lesson. A kid could go to the bathroom, provided a hall pass was in hand—supervision, in a way. But to leave a room full of the young to their own curious momentum, armed with art supplies, scissors even, that was A+ incompetence.

Outside, the wind iced right through my shirt, my tie whipping over my shoulder. I covered my ears with my hands. A snowflake hit me in the eye. *Reindeer. Rhinoceros. Rubberneck.* They could draw all day without having to utilize another letter of the alphabet. *Rocket. Regress.* For some reason, I got down on the ground. *Remorse.* Snow melted under my collar. I pulled my legs to my chest, curled up and tucked my head into my arms as best I could, letting the weather pelt my back. A dog could stay out, get drifted over until the clouds lifted, and then shake it all off.

Back inside, my clothes dripped, and my wet shoes squeaked on the tiling. Mrs. Merriam, the kindergarten teacher, stepped into the hallway. She moved toward me, took off her glasses. "You're steaming," she said.

I looked at my hands. I said, "An experiment."

School was let out just after lunch, but I stayed a while looking through the stack of R sketches. Mrs. Merriam brushed aside my goodbye as she left. None of the drawings made sense: stick people and houses and nice lawns did not begin with the letter R, or even have R in their spellings. Nevertheless, those were the pictures I took home to Sara because I thought she'd enjoy them. Some of the children just drew giant circles, one on top of the other. I placed a gold star sticker on each of those because at least a circle was *round*.

On the way home, I stopped to return the movie. Borucki's would never close for a snowstorm. They were dependable, *reliable*. My hair had been messed up from wearing a stocking cap, and I tried to straighten it some before I got out of the car. When I walked in, Mrs. Borucki was changing the payout on the jackpot sign. I'd never bought a lottery ticket before Sara and I had moved, but everyone in Elkton played the game and Mrs. Borucki was careful to make sure you knew what the numbers to the winners were. So I picked up a ticket nearly each time I stopped there, but I never told Sara about them and promised Mrs. Borucki that if I won I'd split it with her, though I wouldn't have.

After browsing long enough to eat a pear that I hadn't paid for, I found a movie about dog sledding. Teaching was easy: the video was animated. At the rental sheet, I noticed Rita's name just above mine. I asked Mrs. Borucki for a pen to write it down, but I was already holding one.

Rita's kennel wasn't far. I looked up the address in the phone book after I'd returned home. Then I told Sara I had to take *A Bug's Life* back to Borucki's, carrying the new movie with my hand over the title. I had no good answer for why. I could have told Sara the truth, at least about that trip. She would only have asked to come along. But I knew that I did not want to share Rita with Sara. I did not want Sara to interpret me for Rita, or comment on me, and I did not want Sara to be asking all those things about the dogs that she and I had wondered before. I did not want her around, and I see now that it was mostly because I believed she was to blame for everything, even my lying to her.

The snow lightened as I drove. Rita's road hadn't been plowed, so I tried to stay in the only other pair of tire tracks. I followed them at each turn, all the way up the long driveway, along the pasture where a pair of horses stood ass to the wind.

At Rita's truck, where the tire tracks ended, a dog was chained to a cable that stretched from the front to back bumper. Other dog chains segmented the cable, but only one of those lengths was occupied. The dog turned circles in the same spot, over and over, barking at me. The dog's eyes were different colors—one black, one blue. I wasn't sure if I should get out of my car.

I rolled down the window and tilted my head half out and whistled lamely. The dog stood on its hind legs, swatting the air, whining louder. Hidden behind some trees, the rest of the kennel joined in and began barking as a chorus, louder than my car's heater on high defrost.

A small camper trailer, the kind made for the bed of a pickup, rested on stacks of cinder blocks near the edge of the woods. The picnic table in front of the trailer was pitched in a drift. I walked away from Rita's truck, that dog pulling hard against his line and following, the snow filling my shoes. I knocked on the trailer's door, and then checked to see if it was unlocked.

Nothing moved inside, nor did the handle. The horses had not moved either, and past them, across the road where I hadn't noticed, a ginseng farm canopied the hillside. I looked back toward her truck and saw that the dog had its attention elsewhere. One trail led toward the kennel, while the other went out into the land. I knew she was out in that land, and I started heading her way, only to turn back a few steps later.

Instead I walked as far into the kennel as the trail allowed, until I reached a metal gate that separated me from the dogs. Flood lamps hung from fence poles and trees. Some of the dogs stood on top of their houses, plastic fifty-gallon barrels with squared-out openings and flat wooden roofs. Some of the dogs jumped from the housetops to the snow, back to the housetops, to the snow, testing the chains they were clipped to. Some stood still, some sat on their haunches. All of them, they never stopped barking.

Rita did not show in the time I waited for her. My briefcase was still on the car floor. I tore a corner off Lisa Anderson's R picture and wrote a note to Rita on the back of it, asking if she'd come speak to the kids about dog sledding. *The kids would love it.* I left our home number.

I walked to the dogless side of the truck, noticed the pee spots left in the snow. A blanket covered the bench seat in the cab, and the dashboard looked dusty. A pair of mittens, a green thermos. I folded the note lengthwise, so it would fit better under her windshield wiper and not get taken off by the wind.

❧

I DROPPED THE layers of lasagna into a clear Pyrex tray. One half of the filling was thicker than the other, the center a crater. I hadn't even stuck to a consistent building order. Sara leaned against the counter. She'd put the drawings I'd brought her on the refrigerator. With a butter knife, she skewered pickles out of a jar and ate all but the final one, which she fed to me as I added the last shred of mozzarella and pinched the tinfoil tight. A large piece of dill floated in the pickle jar and she knifed it out, sucking the juice.

Sara ran the water for the first round of dishes, and I told her to come sit. "I'll do them later," I said. She squeezed a line of soap into the sink, and when the suds billowed over the brim I asked her again.

"Is this our quality time?" she asked, headed toward me. She wiped her hands on the towel. She had smooth, translucent skin. She stood beside me, putting a hand on the back of my neck. She tossed the towel on the counter, and it slid too far, a corner falling into the dishwater.

Sara poured me some wine, herself some cranberry juice, and I noticed her soft face, her chin, her chubby cheeks. I saw how she—sweating, a little preoccupied, tired and sore—was glowing. More than anything, she was aglow.

"Are you laughing at me?" she asked.

I wasn't even laughing.

"It's for me," I said, squeezing right past her as the phone rang.

Rita said she'd bring Lego, one of her old lead dogs. "He's run thousands of miles," she said. She mentioned feeding, cleaning up her kennel, running her team.

"It's supposed to be cold tomorrow," I said, not knowing how else to chat.

"That's best," she said.

❧

SARA ALWAYS PUT forth a theory that men lacked foresight, but I was sure that, on occasion, I had practiced some forward looking. I skipped breakfast and drank more coffee than I should have, and I went in early on the day of Rita's presentation. On my drive in to school, I stopped at the library in the back of Borucki's. I found no good selections pertaining to dog sledding, except, of course, *The Call of the Wild*, which I'd never read before and which, I thought, would make me appear predictable. But I grabbed it, along with a slim volume entitled *Dogs* that was solely composed of color illustrations of various breeds all in the same posture.

I sat at my desk, the overhead lights droning. Even though the first bus was only just arriving, I pulled out the record book and marked everyone in attendance. Later, when I handed back the children's drawings, I told Lisa how sorry I was that a piece of hers was missing; I explained how I'd thought it was something else and tore off a grocery list from it, and I was terribly sorry, but really hers was probably the best drawing of all. She looked like she was about to cry, so I brought her another congratulatory star and stuck it next to her first. Before Rita arrived, we broke out the art supplies again, but the kids needed direction. I said, "Draw the cold."

Lego was amazing. He never tugged against the leash, and he sat with just the slightest word from Rita. His fur was white with patches of black, almost like a Holstein. "Let him lick your hand," she said.

"Will he bark?" I asked. "I don't want to disturb the other classes."

"Dogs sometimes bark," she said. Her jacket smelled of engine oil.

As soon as I showed Rita into my classroom, Lego leading the way, the kids came to life, unable to stay silent and sitting. "Raise your hand," I said, "if you know what dog sledding is."

"It's best to think like a dog," Rita began. She walked Lego back and forth across the front of the room.

I'd pulled out my desk chair, and slid it to the back corner, as far away as I could get from her. She wore a heavy cable sweater, a pair of denim overalls, scuffed brown boots. She talked patiently with the kids, encouraging their excitement however disruptive it was. She gave the commands for driving a team, explained how "gee" meant right, "haw" left, how "dig dig" would get them to run harder. I needed Sara to be taking notes.

At the end of the presentation, everyone was given a chance to pet Lego, and some of us even tried to hug him. Lunch period was approaching, and I told all the kids to sit back down and see if they could incorporate what they'd just learned into their snow scenes. Only a few listened and moved towards their desks. The rest continued stroking Lego's thick fur, Lego shaking his thick tail.

"Would you?" Rita handed me the leash so she could put on that parka.

"The kids had a blast."

"No one ever asked me to do something like this before, in a school."

"I have to work hard to keep their attention, but they'll be talking about this for the rest of the week."

She let me walk Lego to the front door. "Is that it?" I asked, nodding toward her truck, the sled on top. The sky was pearl, the snow the same, the truck's paint job like a misplaced sun. I suddenly felt like concealing my hands. "It's a fascinating sport," I said. "Do you call it a sport?"

"It's more just how I live." She took Lego's leash back. She ran her hand the length of his tail. "Come take a ride on a sled sometime," she said. "Then you can tell me what to call it."

✥

I TOLD SARA that I was going to go help Mrs. Merriam snow blow her driveway. I'd already let Principal Donwood know that I might be a few minutes late because our furnace was being serviced.

"I'll get up with you," Sara said, struggling to sit up. The sun had hours before rising.

When I asked her, Sara showed me exactly where, in which box, my extra winter clothes had been stowed away. I still hadn't done much unpacking. Unpacking was that much closer to staying. The box revealed snow bibs, a turtleneck, more long underwear, the thick gloves I was looking for, extra socks, another turtleneck, and my old goggles.

So I grabbed the goggles, the gloves. "Maybe these," I said, pulling the bibs out by the cuffs, "to keep my pants clean."

Sara made me a thermos of hot chocolate to take and walked me to the door. The morning sky was ink black, the constellations twinkling horizon to horizon. The stars twinkled, the frost twinkled. The belt from Sara's robe was missing, and she held the front closed with her arms wrapped around herself as best she could. "Jesus," she said, "it's freezing." My cheeks, the tip of my nose, they already stung. I wanted to believe that Sara would just go back to bed after I left, but I knew that once she was up, she was up. I wanted to believe many things I knew weren't true. I took the plastic shovel from the doorstep and threw it in the backseat.

Rita smiled when she saw me, but didn't stop working. The big lights in the trees were almost blinding. There was so much barking I could hardly hear myself when I said hello.

Two sleds sat side by side, and some of the dogs had been harnessed to them. The dogs were in a fury, squirming at the collars, getting into little fights with one another. Rita tried to walk by me, bringing a dog over from its barrel house, and I stepped in her way trying to get out of it. Rita reached out her hand, and I flinched.

"Hey," she said, laughing. "You can help. See over there? Drag that water jug over here. We'll get their soup ready and go." Soup: *hot water, dry dog food, frozen beef.*

Rita gave me a short lesson on the parts of the sled, the way to slow down and not overrun the team, how to steer, how to always weight the inside runner around a corner. I'd remembered the commands from her talk at school.

"You say whoa when you want them to stop pulling, but they probably won't listen." The horizon was yellowing faintly. A woodpecker flew down, stealing a piece of meat out of a dog's bowl.

"You all right?" she asked.

She put Lego in one of my lead positions, six dogs to my team. As soon as the dogs were hooked to the gang line, they wanted to go. Only a short rope tied to a post held my sled from being whisked away. They knew what they were in for. Rita told me to go ahead and get on the sled, my feet square on the runners, knees bent like she'd instructed. The team jerked forward into their harnesses as much as they could, and the front of my sled jumped off the ground. "Are you sure about this?" I asked.

"What do you think, Lego?" Rita yelled above the barking. "Lego says you'll be fine."

After Rita put the last dog on her gang line, she gave me a thumbs-up. I shrugged my shoulders. "This is it," she said.

I pulled my goggles into position. I was terrified, which was terrific. A moment after she released her team, I reached down to my snub line and did the same. The dogs took off and ran ferociously, up the hills, around the corners. My goggles were hard to see through, but I couldn't put a foot on the drag to slow my team down. My body was already tensed for the crash.

As we rode ahead, the sun crested the trees. I repeated the commands Rita gave her team, yelling to my trusty Lego. "On by! On by!" Pass the turn, run straight.

To ease up on the dogs, we walked the longer hills, though Rita ran with her team, while I only jogged at best. When they were working, the dogs did not bark. The only noise was the gentle sound of the sled's runners skimming over the trail. Sometimes Lego, or one of the other dogs, tongue hanging out of its mouth, would glance back at me with a look that I could not interpret. Rita checked on me, too, always with a questioning thumbs-up. Into the distance, as far as I could see, the woods went on in a pale pattern of birch and snow. Thumbs-up, I replied, each time.

In the middle of a long straightaway, Rita stopped the teams and then set out our snow hooks and kicked them in. She told me to keep a foot on my brake. I didn't even take my hands off the sled's handle.

"This is being a musher," she said, one foot still on my snow hook.

"You get to do *this*," I said. "It's amazing."

"You like it?"

"I feel like a mountain man," I said. "Or an Eskimo. I'm in the middle of the woods, surrounded by miles of snow. It's like I want to howl."

"Rrr-wooo," she said.

Some of my dogs began to wander off the trail, jerking my sled to the side, bumping me into the softness of Rita's parka. "Hey," Rita yelled, "line out!" Her breath smelled like coffee and Cheerios. "Dogs," she said, "they're a little dumb sometimes."

AFTER THE RUN, we left the teams hitched to the sleds and fed them their soup. Some of the dogs drank heavily and stole from their neighbor's portion. Rita scolded the stealers and encouraged the meek to drink. They had a tendency, she said, to dehydrate.

When Rita removed the harnesses from the dogs, she let me take some of them back to their barrels. Old, calm dogs, like Lego, walked slowly back to their chains, stood still while I made sure they were locked to their collars. The younger ones stirred impatiently, making it difficult to unsnap them from their lines. They had so much strength that I had to hold them up by the collar, their front legs off the ground, and make them hop alongside me. One still left me on my ass and ran out of the kennel.

"Don't worry about it," Rita said, after she'd finally chased the dog down, catching him at some bloody snow by the soup bucket. "They even do it to me sometimes."

I brought out the hot chocolate and told Rita that I still had time before I had to be at school. While she finished with the dogs, I explained how I was chilled. How I needed to sit down. How this was all new to me.

The trailer was small, and the heater inside sounded a heavy, electrical hum as the fan blew round. We sat at the table, Rita across from me. Lego was with us, and he sat with me for a while, leaning into me, pressing me into the veneered wall. His breath did not smell like hers, and the hot chocolate was overly sweet and not very warm. At times, Lego put his head back and lolled out his tongue so that it was right there—hot, humid, in my face. If I leaned into him, he only pushed against me more.

"Lego," I said, looking to Rita for help, "I can hardly breathe."

"You can tell him to get down if you want."

"Go on," I said. "Get down." When he didn't, all she had to do was snap her fingers.

Rita's bottom lip stuck for an instant on that crooked tooth of hers whenever she smiled, and it did it again. She took off her wool hat and set it on the table between us. Her hair was matted down, and after she scruffed it out, it took an even wilder, more alluring form. "Hat head," she said, scratching. "Itches."

I grabbed Rita's hat from the middle of the table and pulled it over to my side before sliding it back at her. It crumpled softly into her forearm. Instead of giggling coyly, instead of catching her lip on another smile, which was supposed to be what happened, Rita seemed surprised and somewhat put off by what I'd done, and I got the sense that I'd been childish in her eyes.

"It's a great hat," I said.

"Does the job."

"I'm sure," I said, "I was just—"

She faked sliding the hat back at me, and I slapped the table. "Were you?" she asked.

My watch read nine-thirty, an hour past when I should've been back. I still had a twenty-minute drive in front of me. Since finishing with the dogs, I'd felt unbound. It felt as if I hadn't just run them in a big circle that ended where it began, but instead had taken them on a long, straight marathon, to a place far in the distance, so far away that there was no going back. With Rita's look, I suddenly remembered what was what, and that I had a job, and that I had a wife, and that I had lied.

"Lego, can I see you again sometime?" I asked, standing to leave.

"What's that, Lego?" Rita said, smiling as I gave the dog a last pat on the rump. "You say sure, as long as he lets me make the hot chocolate."

❧

WHEN I GOT home after work that night, Sara met me at the front door. Principal Donwood had called that morning, looking for me, two hours late. Sara didn't know anything about a broken furnace or an appointment with a repairman, and she told Principal Donwood what she knew, which was that I'd left early for Mrs. Merriam's. Sara had been surprised to learn that I wasn't at work. Then she was worried.

"You know," Sara told me as I stood there, waiting to go inside, "he was saying, 'There's probably a simple explanation,' and I was thinking, yeah, Brian crashed the car, he went off the road. He's hurt. He's bleeding. That's simple."

Principal Donwood had already filled me in on all these matters— how he'd called Sara, how Mrs. Merriam hadn't a clue what Sara was talking about—as I was reprimanded in his office. Anthony Peters, freckle-faced and yawning, and in trouble for copying answers, sat next to me through the whole ordeal. When Principal Donwood asked Anthony, after asking me the very same question, if two hours was not the same as a little bit late, Anthony had to admit what I'd had to. "No," he said, "it's not."

Sara held the door open with her right foot. She wore a pair of my old wool socks. I set our plastic shovel at the base of the porch, the snow an icy block too hard to push into. The lights were on in the front hallway, and I could feel the warmth slipping out, cutting the chill. I held the empty thermos in one hand, along with my briefcase, my snow bibs hanging in the other.

"What was I supposed to think?" she asked.

I stared at her feet, trying to find something to say. I'd had the entire day to come up with an excuse. "I don't know," I said. "You weren't supposed to think anything."

❧

I RAN WITH Rita one more time. I called from school and told her how much fun I'd had, how I couldn't stop trying to remember the sensation of being on that sled—the glide, the speed, the sound of the snow under the rails, which was a sound much like a finger running over soft corduroy. She agreed to let me try again.

Lego was at my lead, once more, and we rode on the same trail—two laps. As we crossed the field just outside the kennel, the western horizon opened and we could see the sun setting, marking the bend of the earth in oranges and reds. When we finished, we fed the dogs and put them away, and I didn't land on my rear, nor let anything slip.

"Still like it?" Rita asked.

We were standing next to each other, and I grabbed her by the waist and kissed her on the cheek and acted overwhelmed to get away with it. "I don't think I'll ever forget this," I proclaimed. "I think I'm a convert."

I offered to take Rita out for dinner. Instead, she invited me back to her cabin so she could take care of the rest of her dogs.

"Name something," she said, "I'll cook."

We stopped at Borucki's on the way home from the kennel. Rita parked right in front of the door, and I waited in my car while she ran in, but then I decided that I should buy us something to drink. When the bell rattled they both looked at me, though Mrs. Borucki didn't stop counting change.

"Hey," Rita said, "what's up?"

"Look who's here," Mrs. Borucki said, as I waved at Rita. "One of your students was just in. Mrs. Anderson and her daughter."

Rita had a smile on her face, as did Mrs. Borucki, which made me think that Mrs. Borucki could see what was going on. But I decided then that Mrs. Borucki wouldn't be smiling if she knew, she'd be scowling. She thought the world of Sara and was always telling me what a lucky guy I was to have her.

"Lisa's a sweetheart," I said. "One of my best students."

I pointed toward the refrigerator that held the sodas, the milk, the other dairy products. "I was just thinking about getting something to drink," I said to Rita and Mrs. Borucki both.

I could see Rita's reflection warped and colored blue in the cooler's glass. Mrs. Borucki floated behind her. I had no idea what I was doing, so I grabbed the refrigerator's handle to make it seem like I was getting close to a decision. I pulled open the door a little and let it suck shut. I pulled open the door a little and let it shut again, trying to pretend there was nothing behind me. Rita rolled up her newspaper and tapped it on the counter.

"Until tomorrow," she said to Mrs. Borucki.

"See you then, dear."

After the front door chimed and closed, I turned and looked at Rita walking through the glow cast from the store's windows. When she got in her truck she glanced up before she started playing with the radio. The motor for the cooler next to me snarled to a stop. Behind me hung the sign for the lottery jackpot, and I read the backward numbers off the reflection in the glass. We were talking hundreds of millions. I glanced at my own reflection, and then thought it wiser to look away.

"Give me two," I said to Mrs. Borucki, while pointing at the lottery display. I set the cider and beer on the counter and got out my money.

"This could be it," she said excitedly, shaking the tickets at me. "This could be our lucky day."

RITA LEANED OUT of bed and turned on a lamp, then reached into her nightstand and handed me a condom. I sat up, the blanket falling around my waist. I pushed the circle around inside the package. I hadn't used one in years and could feel myself shrinking.

The nightstand was too far to reach, so I tucked the wrapper under a pillow. I couldn't tell which side was which and started rolling the condom on upside down. Rita reached between her legs, pushing against herself while she rubbed my back with her other hand. I was sitting with my legs straight out in front of me, and I was bent over myself, and even after I'd turned the condom over it still seemed like it wasn't right, like I was rolling against the roll.

Rita kept a few dogs at home, and they surrounded the bed. As I struggled, I met eyes with one of them, who stood up and came over to see what was happening. When the dog started sniffing at me, I hissed at it like a cat.

"Hey!" Rita said, slapping me on the shoulder. "Go on!" she said to her dog. "Out!"

Rita put her arms around me and pulled me back down. She took the condom and dropped it on the floor, and when another of the dogs went for it, she gently swatted it on the head and said no. I pulled the blankets back over us. When another ruined but unused condom lay on the floor, and the dogs came to smell again, she shooed them away once more.

I kept pawing, until she finally said stop and told me not to worry.

SARA WAS ASLEEP when I came home. I'd told her I was going to stay at school until I finished some lesson plans. After brushing my teeth and dropping my clothes in a pile in the bathroom, I crawled into bed and slept back to back with her.

In the morning, I gave Sara the lottery ticket I'd bought for Rita. She was scrambling me eggs. I'd been trying to look engaged with my briefcase and getting ready for work when I found the ticket in my pants pocket. My expression must have changed, because Sara asked what it was that I was holding.

"This," I said. "It's for you." I passed her the ticket, taking the spatula in return and fixing my dish. "But you have to split it with me," I said.

Neither of ours was a winner. No one hit the jackpot that round, and the stakes went up. The jackpot became a regular news item. Sara wanted to play again and kept asking me to bring home another ticket. I hadn't gone to Borucki's since being there with Rita. I drove out of my way to avoid it. Finally, on the eve of the drawing, Sara—bundled up and holding her purse—walked out the front door just as I pulled into the driveway after school.

"We're leaving," she yelled, coming up to the car. Once inside, she bounced in her seat a little. "I want to go to Borucki's."

While Sara bought the tickets, I hid in the library. I sat on the one small stool and gazed out past the books and into the row of baby food and diapers. I could hear Mrs. Borucki and Sara talking about the forecast, clear and cold.

"Honey," Sara shouted back to me, "we need anything else?"

The sound of the cash register covered the sound of the front door, and when I stood up to leave, I noticed Rita's truck at the gas pumps. She was already inside, waiting behind Sara.

"Hi," Sara said, zipping shut her purse and stepping out of Rita's way. Myself, I hadn't moved.

"Sara, wait," Mrs. Borucki said. "Have you met Rita?"

Sara asked Rita all those things she'd been curious about—the types of dogs, the speed at which they ran—though I'd learned those answers already and should have told her.

"It's nice to have met you," Sara said.

Rita reached out her hand, and she and Sara shook. "Nice to meet you."

When Sara had waited long enough at the front door, she called over to me, asking if I was ready or what.

"Brian," Rita said as I approached the cash register.

I stopped in front of her, unable to speak.

Rita had her mittens stuffed under an armpit. The collar of her parka's hood wore a dusting of quickly melting snow. "You've a lovely wife."

I looked at Sara, who looked happy. "Yes," I said, beginning to walk away. "Sara's great."

"I can tell," Rita said to my back.

Sara's smile had widened. "He's not so bad, either."

"Of course," Rita said. "Of course."

Outside, on the back of Rita's truck, Lego and some others were riding in their boxes. Sara went up to them and started cooing. The snow had stopped falling, though the bitter wind was still blowing it around. Lego lay curled and uninterested, though others stood and barked at us. "They're so cute," Sara said. She held out her hand to a box, so the dog inside could sniff. "I want one."

"If you win the lottery," I told Sara, towing her toward the car.

Sara pulled against my arm, stopping me in my tracks. "When I win the lottery?" she asked, perked up, wanting a promise.

"When we win the lottery."

Stargazer
autumn 1957

AS THE PICKUP truck approached, Walters raised his free hand and motioned for the vehicle to stop. In his other hand he clutched the stock of a lever-action Winchester, the gun barrel angled over his shoulder. Behind him stood two sawhorses, one in each lane of the highway.

Mike had known Walters for thirty years, so he was both surprised, and not, by the roadblock.

"There's a toll now," Walters said.

"Toll?" Mike asked. "Just move them sawhorses."

"It's a quarter per person," he said. "Or animal," he added, noting Copper, Mike's dog.

Mike pointed to the edge of the road. "There's enough space I can just drive around."

Walters shrugged. "Maybe."

Across the highway, a layer of fog still clung to the river. The night had been cold, and the sun had yet to crest the tree line. A patch of October frost bisected the roof of Walters's tavern, the Stargazer. A large neon sign—a green comet with a trail of orange sparks—hummed on the façade. Next to the tavern, Walters had a little store where he sold a few things like kerosene and fishing line and fresh eggs. He still sold jars of maple syrup bottled by Mike's wife.

"You're going to shoot me over fifty cents?" Mike asked.

Though Mike had turned his radio down, Walters could still hear

Kitty Wells singing about the lonely side of town. "You come in, buy a cup of coffee, order some breakfast," Walters said, "I'll forget the toll."

"That deal apply just to me, or is that how it works for everyone?"

"It's an off-season tax. You don't have to eat if you don't want to."

"Walters, get out of the way."

Walters shifted his rifle and held out a hand for the money. He looked Mike straight in the eyes, and Mike studied him, searching for some clue as to whether or not Walters knew how ridiculous he was being.

Walters wore his blue-and-black flannel coat buttoned up to the collar. He had plump, red cheeks scribbled with spider veins. His eyes looked overinflated. The Brylcreem in his hair made it seem darker than it was, but his sideburns, flecked with gray, told the truth. For a moment he considered discounting the rate for Copper, but then just as quickly reversed himself and thought about charging more. Mike hadn't been to the Stargazer in over a decade, and the way Walters saw it, that made Mike one part prudent, two parts piece of shit.

"Fifty cents now," Walters said, "or a dollar when you come back through." He took his receipt booklet from his breast pocket, ready to start a balance sheet. "You can even pay ahead, if you want credit."

Mike slipped his truck into gear, and the transmission engaged with a hard *thunk*. "This isn't your best idea," he said to Walters. "I can't think anyone's going to let this skate very long."

It was an idea, though. Summer had passed, and the river was low and warm. The land had emptied itself of tourists, and hunting season was still a month away. The only customer Walters could count on was Irvin Klomatski, who came every two weeks to spend some of his pension check. Irvin was eighty-seven, and couldn't drink but two drafts, which he'd milk for hours.

"Are you going to pay?" Walters asked. "Or owe?"

"Send me a bill," Mike said, pulling onto the shoulder. After he rolled up his window, he pawed Copper's head and said, "Dog, that man's a fool."

❧

By eight-thirty, the sun had melted the frost from the Stargazer's roof, and Walters had tired of waiting. He left the sawhorses in place and took his rifle inside, standing it next to the tavern's front door. After the bathroom, he made another pot of coffee and lit the griddle. He wiped down the bar, then walked to the front window and turned on the *Open* sign, pulling too hard on the string and breaking it. Walters tried tying the sun-faded cord back together, but he grew frustrated working with something so small, and he left it on the windowsill.

Walters pulled out a stool and sat down with his back to the bar, eyes on the road. He could hear his wife, Tooty, vacuuming upstairs. Rhythmic frump fumps played across the ceiling as she worked. He'd bought her the Electrolux for her birthday, and she loved it—she could drag it along, and it just followed behind. Walters, on the other hand, felt differently. The vacuum cleaner, Walters thought, was going to break him.

The vacuum's sound was like a splinter; once its electric whir got into him, Walters had a hard time getting it out. The noise nearly eclipsed his ability to think. Sometimes, when his wife was vacuuming, Walters just found himself standing there—humming a single, flat note.

Walters got up, shut down the stove, and locked the cash register. He let the *Open* sign be and went out to his car. He drove south, stopping at his sawhorses and dragging them apart, wide enough so that anyone could pass between.

❧

WALTERS TURNED OFF at the Boy Scout camp and then skirted the property on a two-track road, scraggly poplar and birch pressing in on both sides. When the road forked, Walters followed the cut that veered away from the river. Most of the leaves had dropped, but a few brown curls still decorated the branches. Walters drove at an idle, windows open, weaving the Chieftain through the woods as far as it could go. When the road finally rutted out along a steep climb, he parked and walked from there.

He had almost reached his derelict still when the bear cub startled him. He wasn't sure what it was at first, only that it had clawed its way up the white pine in four or five noisy strides. Could've been a porcupine, except they weren't hardly as quick.

He was surprised his heart was racing like it was. He locked his eyes on the dark lump and tried willing the animal to move so that he could see its silhouette. He remembered a time deer hunting, when he'd been plagued by the quiet sense that someone was watching, only to look up hours later and see that a great horned owl had been sitting above him all morning. Now he could see that it was a black bear. The cub cried out, plaintive and mule-like, a cry it had been making for days, and Walters ducked as if something had been thrown at him.

Walters had smelled the sow on the walk in, though he hadn't known what the stench was exactly. Dead something. A logging truck pulling pulpwood off state land had hit her. Now Walters scanned the woods, trying to see through the tangle of trees. Walters moved closer to the cub, squatting down so he could get a better sightline.

The cub was about twenty feet up, clinging. Its hind legs were planted underneath itself, its front legs splayed out along the bark. The cub's coat had the same dull sheen as dirty oil, but its muzzle was brown, and there were faint brown markings above its eyes. He had never been so close to a bear before, and they had never seemed so odd to him—the cub looked so stuck, Walters had trouble thinking of it as a bear. It seemed more like a tailless dog, or some child in a costume. Its round ears, like little black dishes, made Walters think of Mickey Mouse.

When the cub began crying again, Walters hustled away. "You're as bad as a vacuum," he said, stumbling over some deadfall. The cub was nearly bleating—"Eeh, eeh, eeh."

❧

WALTERS WAS IN the storeroom getting the birdseed for Tooty's feeders and didn't hear the car. The screen door creaked open, and then thwacked shut. Walters listened to see if it was Klomatski, and could tell by the hammer of footsteps it wasn't.

"One second," Walters shouted down the hallway, digging an empty coffee can into the sack of sunflower seeds. He filled the can to overflowing and then poured some off. He rolled the top of the sack closed and pushed the bag back to its spot. Two men spoke in the bar, though he couldn't hear what they were saying. "I'm coming," Walters said, not realizing that they wouldn't be able to hear him either.

Walters made a couple of stewed-pork sandwiches for the two men, garnishing each plate with pickles he'd canned himself. A small pass-through joined the kitchen with the barroom, and when the plates were ready, Walters slid them onto the serving ledge and rang a bell. He walked out of the kitchen and around to the bar, picked up the dishes, and took them to his customers.

"Smells good," the younger-looking man said. He wore a brand-new fishing vest and reeked of cologne. He had a nose that reminded Walters of an egret.

"Refills?" Walters asked. He had one tap: Blatz.

The second man asked Walters if the road was closed. He said they'd wanted to get down to the reservation for some fishing.

"That?" Walters asked, pointing at his roadblock. The man nodded, his mouth busy with the sandwich. "I don't know what that is," Walters said. "I just haven't had time to pull them out of the way, is all. Bored kids, I guess."

Walters enjoyed talking to the men. He told them about the cub, and they both shook their heads, saying they couldn't imagine. The two men were young enough that they called Walters Old-Timer, and old enough that Walters didn't take offense when they did.

"Pretty late for brookies," Walters said. "If you find some deep pools you might be able to get a few rainbows."

"Know any spots?" the egret asked, pulling the napkin from his shirt collar and cleaning his hands. He had a squared head, a cropped haircut, cheeks that looked as if they were stuffed.

"Know of plenty," Walters said. "But not many I want to talk about. You buy a map, I can point a couple out to you."

"Worms?"

"There's a place down by County M. He just digs them out of his garden."

The two men each left a nickel tip, and Walters considered it fine. They walked over to the sawhorses and moved them off the road. Besides the map, the fishermen had also bought a bottle of schnapps, and Walters chuckled as they uncapped it in the parking lot. The men were likely to stumble in a rapid and drown, or put a hook through one of their ears. They lowered the top on their convertible. The backseat held enough stuff for a month of fishing.

As the car bounced its way onto the road, the wind pushed a few yellow leaves along the asphalt. The blue sky was streaked with cirrus clouds, and like everyone else, Walters feared what might suddenly fall from it, atomizing them all. He noticed that he'd never put his rifle away, and he wondered if the men had seen.

❧

EARLY THE NEXT morning, this time armed, Walters returned to his still. He followed his nose and found the bloated sow, her gray tongue sagging from her mouth. Not far away, near the same pine where it had been treed yesterday, the cub dug at a rotting log. When it noticed Walters, instead of running, the little bear sat on its haunches and almost wobbled over.

"Don't worry," Walters said, taking a flask filled with sugar water from his back pocket. He made soft, clicking noises, the same calls he used to bring the cats to dinner. "You can trust me," he said, which was mostly true. "Here," he whispered, slowly moving closer, offering a taste.

The cub had bits of crusty pus in the corners of its eyes, and its nose looked dried out. Each time Walters took a step forward, the bear hopped backward. Walters had gone through a similar thing with a milking cow he'd once had, but then he just threw a rope around her neck and dragged her back to the stall. Why the hell hadn't he thought to bring a rope?

Walters sat beside a stump and decided to wait for the bear to come to him, but the warm sunlight and the quiet of the woods made him drowsy. He woke from his nap when he felt the cub licking his hand. The cub's tongue was rough and wet, and Walters shuddered from its touch. His rifle lay across his lap, his arms folded over the top. The flask was at his side, swarmed by ants where it had leaked. The cub turned part of the way around, ready to run, to start its little game again. Walters made a grab and caught the bear by a hind leg—the leg stretched long, trying to jerk away.

Walters didn't open for business that day. The two fishermen pounded on the door, sure that they could see someone inside. They had to go all the way to Elkton for lunch.

Walters closed all the doors to the barroom, pushed aside the tables and stools, and set the animal in the clearing. He had wrapped the cub in his jacket, then doubled the padding by adding a blanket he'd found in the trunk. Walters's arms, crosshatched with the cuts and bites he'd gotten while capturing the cub, still throbbed and stung.

"Are you as hungry as me?" Walters asked as he loosened the fabric. He'd already un-gunked the bear's eyes with it. They reminded him of obsidian.

Walters pulled a quart of buttermilk from the refrigerator and poured some into a mixing bowl. The bear sniffed at it cautiously. Soon it started drinking, then slurping, painting its snout in white. When the bowl was empty the cub skidded it around the room, trying to lick out every last drop. The bear sat down, wiped its nose with its paws, and then licked those paws clean.

A few seconds later, as it would do nearly each of those early feeds, the cub threw everything right back up.

⁂

TOOTY HAD ROLLED over and put her back to him, and Walters was now trying to melt her. He snuggled up close, his hard-on nestled against her rear. He ran a hand along her side, his calluses catching on her nightgown. "I've got a *big* surprise for you," he said, unable to resist.

Tooty sighed. Walters's surprises were often disasters. She scooted her butt away from him, but Walters followed. She worked herself to the edge of the bed, and thought about rolling off. She acted as if she had fallen asleep.

"This is going to really tickle you," Walters said. "You're going to just scream. When you see it, I know it, you're going to scream."

Tooty could feel Walters leaning over and wanting a reaction.

"It'll be a hoot," he said. "You're going to think it's adorable."

Tooty thought maybe she should roll over for Walters. If she gave him something tonight, she'd have better leverage tomorrow, and it was sounding like tomorrow was going to be worse than tonight.

"You can help me name it," he said.

She guessed he'd bought another boat. He already had three stored in the backyard, floating in a lake of unmowed grass. Walters had wanted to start a charter service with the first one, but the boat was too big for the river, and you didn't need a charter service to catch pan fish at the lake. She'd named that one *Bluebird*. The second was *New Susanna*, which was an aluminum rowboat that Walters had rented out to tourists until he tired of always having to trailer it, never trusting anyone else to transport the thing. The third boat, a trawler, hadn't gotten a name, but had gone straight to the field. She still didn't know what it was for.

Tooty went on pretending to sleep, and finally, Walters let her be.

Walters went outside. Restless—he wanted to see how the cub was doing. He'd spent the afternoon cleaning out the old dog pen. He'd been using it to store lumber ever since Rascal, the weak-hipped Labrador Mike sold him, died of heartworm. Walters had stacked the scrap wood in piles according to length on the lawn, had swept the cement slab clean, sending clouds of dust drifting toward the road. He'd walked out back to his tree farm and collected pine needles and windfall to make the habitat seem a little more natural. He'd filled a stainless steel bowl with water, filled another with honey and bread and a little bit of cooked chicken.

The waning moon was bright enough that Walters didn't really need the flashlight, and after he saw that the old car blanket had been shredded, and that the water and food dishes had been tipped over, and that the bear was fine, Walters turned off the beam and just sat in the moonlight with the cub, letting it lick his face through the fencing. Walters scissored his fingers and made cute, teasing noises. The bear nipped at Walters's cheek, and caught a piece of flesh. Walters supposed he'd probably deserved that.

Walters had made a pie that morning, hoping the fishermen might still be around. "Try this," he said, pushing a small piece of pie crust through the chain link. "Best apple pie around." The next time Walters held the crust higher, so the bear would have to stand to get it. "That's it," Walters said. The cub only came up to his waist. "Reach up. Reach. Reach."

The bear looked so natural on its hind legs, Walters wondered why it didn't always walk upright. The last piece of crust was too small to split, but Walters tried anyway, turning it to crumbs. The bear fell back on its butt, plopped down just like Walters's boy had when he was first figuring how to stand and walk.

Walters sucked a glob of apple from his thumb. He'd grown cold, but was afraid to go back inside, where he'd start wondering what to do with himself. The cub sniffed at the floor, tracking every speck and licking it right up. Walters took a few big sniffs, too, trying to understand the night air like an animal might. Tomorrow there'd be more frost. The stars had that look. The air had a purity that Walters could only associate with water—it was cold and bracing and tasted clean—and it cured his urge to try with Tooty again. He'd grab the afghan and sleep outside.

❧

TOOTY THOUGHT BONKERS would be a good name. "For the both of you," she said, after her husband insisted he was keeping the bear.

"We'll call you Blackjack," Walters said later, after his wife had returned to the living room.

Walters and Blackjack adapted to their new lives quickly. Walters moved the sawhorses from the road and into the backyard, right next to the piles of scrap wood he'd sorted, and started working on improvements to Blackjack's pen. The days were crisp and bright, the road empty. To keep Blackjack from knocking over his food and water bowls, Walters bolted them to a wide hemlock plank. He used an old ceiling beam as a climbing post, and twice had to reinforce the spot where he'd attached it to the fencing so it'd hold against Blackjack's yanking. Whenever Walters went inside the pen with Blackjack he wore a pair of welding gloves and several long-sleeved shirts. Blackjack's claws didn't retract, and they were as needle-like, Walters thought, as a dog's first teeth.

Walters drove over to the Schimell place and picked what blackberries he could get from the thicket. Most were overripe and nearly ruined. When Walters tried hand feeding them to Blackjack, Blackjack got so eager he bruised Walters's hands. On one occasion when Blackjack grew too aggressive and wouldn't stop clawing and biting at Walters's feet, and cornered him in the pen, Walters got scared and kicked him in the chest. Blackjack squealed and went cowering off. Later, when Walters went out to apologize, Blackjack fell asleep in his lap.

Walters drove up the hill to the settlers' cemetery and hiked along the oaks to collect acorns. The gray squirrels scolded him, but the nuts were plentiful. Each acorn he found made Walters feel a little better. He dug through moldy leaves and looked for pieces of rotting wood, pieces burrowed out by beetles and filled with larvae. He gathered all the earth-worms he could find, unsure if Blackjack would even like them.

From the cemetery, Walters followed the fence line all the way to the railroad tracks. He walked east along the tracks for a while, and then cut back toward the road. He passed through a short draw, and then around a thicket of buckthorn, until he was at the far edge of Mike's cornfield. The harvest had occurred long ago, and the stalks had faded and turned brittle, but Walters still found a few salvageable ears to pilfer. He continued along the field, kicking at clods of dirt as he went. The forest pushed right in on this part of the corn, and the ground had a tendency to stay wet, but the chunks of earth turned to powder every time Walters toed one.

At Mike's bait pile, Walters started pitching the apples into the woods. The air smelled slightly of old cider. Slow, docile wasps let Walters steal pieces of fruit right out from under them. Walters wasn't against baiting deer, but he didn't want it to be this easy for Mike. Baiting made hunting a practice of patience, and that bothered Walters, especially since patience was one of his lesser skills. He scattered the pile until he got to the soft, mushy apples at the bottom. Then he marked the area with piss.

The field ended less than a hundred yards from Mike's house. To get from the corn to the road, Walters would have to walk through a patch of open lawn, and then up a ditch. His other option was to go back through the woods and bushwhack.

Walters knew that Mike and the rest of the Vandenhoven clan wouldn't be idle, and he thought he had a good chance of slipping by without being noticed. He thought of running for it, saw himself bounding away in deer-like strides. Then he decided it'd be best to walk. Quickly, yes. But normal, like nothing was out of place.

Walters was halfway to the road when he heard Copper. She was too old to come after him, but she could still bark like hell.

Mike stood on his porch, watching Walters trying to sneak past. He wondered what Walters was up to, but also knew that with Walters it was impossible to guess—it could've been a million ludicrous things at once. "Hey," Mike shouted, cupping his hands to amplify his voice. "I see you!"

The words reached Walters clearly, but he didn't stop. He kept his head down, focused on where he stepped, pretending that it was like walking on hot coals, and that you just had to keep moving to come out fine. Mike let out a piercing whistle, the same one he'd been using for years to signal his children to come in for dinner. Walters knew it'd be hard to believe that he didn't hear it, but he'd deny it anyway if Mike asked.

Walters scrambled up the weedy ditch, dropping an ear of corn. When he hit the road, he turned west and headed toward the cemetery, putting Mike and Copper and all that bother behind.

WALTERS HAD MADE it all the way to Tinkler Creek when Mike pulled up next to him in his truck. Walters kept walking, while Mike idled alongside him. The passenger window was down, and the two men looked at each other, not saying anything. Mike kept glancing in the rearview, making sure nobody came racing up on them.

Walters started walking slower and slower, and Mike matched him, until they'd both come to a stop. Walters leaned against the passenger door of the Studebaker, his forearms pressed hard against the top of the window frame. "You seem to be following me."

"Oh," Mike said, "just seeing what you're up to."

Walters looked around the inside of Mike's truck cab, inspecting it for something, though he didn't know what.

"Was calling after you," Mike said. "Guess you didn't hear."

"Mustn't have."

Mike dropped his head the same way he did when Copper had done something annoying, but cute. He asked if Walters was headed home. "That's a hell of a long walk," he added.

The two men rode in near silence, looking straight ahead. "How about that new stadium?" Mike asked, unable to stand the quiet.

"Well," Walters said, lingering. "I suppose Curly Lambeau was all right by me."

After Tinkler Creek, the shadowy forest changed to a sun-brushed meadow. Walters's car stood out on the horizon. "There it is," Walters said, pointing, in case anyone in earshot happened to be a moron.

Mike turned into the cemetery and drove slowly down the gravel road. There were many of these old, small cemeteries throughout the county, and both men had relatives buried at this one. They were relatives that had passed generations ago, and neither Walters nor Mike had any memory of them. Those they remembered were buried in town, behind St. Joseph's. Mike's young niece—"Sue Ann Wurdinger, 1934–1953"—was buried there. She died in an accident up near Zilbesky's Corner. Walters's boy, Ricky, had been driving the other car.

Mike passed Walters's car and made a U-turn, pulling up so that Walters wouldn't have to walk around. After Ricky had recuperated, after his broken ribs and clavicle and jawbone healed, he tried to stay nearby and make a life of it at the mill, but he drifted away pretty quick, mostly to everyone's relief. These days he was stationed at Camp Ripley, near Little Falls. Walters didn't know how to measure the recent pride he had for Ricky against all the other crap.

"All righty," Mike said, offering what he could. He didn't even mention the corn.

Walters wanted to tell Mike about Blackjack but held back, thinking that if he kept it a secret it was something he owned all his own. "If it was me," Walters said, holding the door handle, "I would've just stayed home, saved yourself the trouble." He had wanted to say thank you.

"If you would've stayed home," Mike said, "that's true. That would have certainly saved me some trouble."

Walters stepped down out of Mike's truck and adjusted his pockets. He thought to explain the corn. "Well, how about this?" Walters asked. "Out of fairness, this can make up for those times you skipped the toll."

Mike didn't really want to hear the rest, nor see how Walters's logic played out, but he couldn't help but ask. "You're collecting your toll in corn?"

"This," Walters said, holding up a cob, "is silage." Mike tried hard to run over his foot, but missed.

❧

IRVIN KLOMATSKI STEPPED out behind the Stargazer to let Walters know he had more customers. It was the end of November, the last weekend of deer season, and Blackjack weighed about fifty pounds now, maybe more. Besides Tooty, Irvin was the only one who knew about Blackjack. "You decide?" he asked Walters.

"He might be," Walters said, quietly latching the pen. The sky was purple, and soon it'd be dark, which Walters didn't quite feel ready for. A dusting of snow covered the ground. The cold snap seemed to have made Blackjack lethargic, and he spent most of the time hidden away in the wooden crate that Walters had modified for him. When Walters put an ear close to the opening of the den box, he heard something of a purr.

"He ain't really snoring," he said, waiting as Irvin labored up the back step. "But he's been sleeping all day."

The bar was more crowded than Walters expected. He'd only heard a few cars pull up, but they obviously had been packed tight. He could tell the men had already been drinking, and guessed by their roughness with one another that they'd probably filled their tags. "Who's ready?" he asked, turning the first glass upright.

Irvin climbed on his barstool, and went back to gumming his lips and watching the show. The hunters had come in two groups, separate from each other, but after a few rounds of drinks they started sharing stories down the bar. Only two men had come out empty so far, a small thing their buddies wouldn't let them forget. Everyone seemed thankful for the snow. One man had tracked his kill for a quarter mile. "Against that white," he said, "I just followed a red line right to her."

At the beginning of hunting season Walters had taped an *Out of Order* sign on the jukebox. Now one of the hunters asked him about it. "Yep," Walters said, thinking things out. He'd put the sign up because with the jukebox going, and with more than a couple people in the bar, it just got too loud for him. Tooty didn't like it upstairs either. "It just doesn't want to play for some reason," he said, as if it was a mystery. "Irvin, though, he's on his second beer. If he keeps going, we might get him to sing for you."

After that the men took to Irvin, and his barstool neighbor even bought him a shot of brandy, which Walters watered down for Irvin's sake. They asked Irvin about his season, and he told them how he didn't hunt anymore—that he no longer had the strength to field-dress a deer, and his eyes weren't as sharp as they used to be, and he hated being cold. Even in the warmth of the bar, Irvin's skin looked papery and vein-blue.

After the second diluted brandy, feeling good and loose and hardly bound by his rust, Irvin told his new friends about Blackjack.

Walters was reluctant to take the men outside, but he finally relented. One man had even put a dollar down saying Walters was full of it, a bet Irvin quickly took. "You should've gone in for more," Walters said to him. "That's free money, Irvin."

The night was sparkling and harsh, the air so cold it altered the men's breathing. The dusting of white that covered the ground was no longer feathery, but icy and brittle under the men's boots. They lined up around the pen, a curtain of hunters. They looked at the water dish, the food bowl, the old tire, the den box, and thought what most would: this is a dog pen.

"He's hibernating," Walters explained.

"Come on," the guy who'd bet the dollar said.

Walters took the man into the pen with him. "Listen," he said, getting down on one knee and motioning the man to do the same. The hunter was still wearing his insulated snow bibs, but the cold concrete cut through Walters's pants. "Put your ear close to the door," Walters said. "Now take a look inside. Tell me that's a dog."

As the man leaned close, one of his buddies outside the pen roared, causing him to scramble back from the box. Even Walters laughed.

"Well?" someone asked after the man had taken a second look.

"Well," the man said, standing up. He opened his billfold. "I never seen or smelled no dog like that."

❧

WHEN THE WEATHER warmed in early December, Blackjack stirred a few times, leaving his den box to eat and drink and defecate, but when the first big blizzard screamed down from Canada right before Christmas, Blackjack returned to his den, taking the time to plug the opening with straw once he was inside. Walters had gone to the trouble of covering the side of the pen with canvas, and the wind rattled it against the fencing. Snow blew underneath and settled in a small drift along the cement. That first storm dropped more than a foot, and Walters spent much of the next day clearing the parking lot and shoveling the walkways, throwing the snow into piles that would build over the winter until they were taller than he was.

On New Year's Eve it was just Walters and Irvin Klomatski, and they sat across from each other at the bar, their heads hung above their drinks—Irvin with a beer, and Walters with a cup of coffee—listening to the radio, waiting for the time to pass. Around eleven, Walters brought out a mason jar of homemade gin, and he poured them both a tumbler. The gin smelled more antiseptic than it tasted, though it had a blunt, gut-warming burn to it, enough so that both Irvin and Walters finished their drink shaking their heads and growling, "Ahhhk."

Walters started spending time in his workshop, trying to catch up on things he'd let slide. He replaced the handle he'd snapped on his digging fork, taking the time to whittle down the throat until it fit just right. He tightened the swivel-joint on the snowplow, and brought the hydraulic oil back up to level. He cut the pieces for some shelves that he'd promised Tooty, and then stood them in the corner, which is where they stayed.

The weather took on a pattern—heavy snows followed by cold winds and blue skies, days that were both frigid and blinding, and drew everyone to the windows. The nights were long and oppressive, and never seemed to grow shorter. By February, the river had frozen completely, and Walters had to drive all the way over to Sawyer Lake to fish, augering through two feet of ice to get to water. On Valentine's Day Walters gave Tooty a silver brooch, a swan, and then in bed that evening pestered her until she let him crawl on top of her and bury his face in her neck.

Walters began working on the sign in March. He took the planks he'd cut for Tooty's shelves and bracketed them together into one big signboard, laying it across the sawhorses so it could be primed and painted. Once the red paint had dried—Walters thought red would stand out the best—he snapped several chalk lines across the wood so that he could keep the lettering straight. He penciled BLACKJACK THE BEAR, and then traced over the letters with yellow paint. Below that, not quite knowing what it would mean, he added SHOWS DAILY.

Then just before St. Patrick's Day, Irvin died in his sleep. Tooty, dressed in black, wearing her new brooch, went to the wake at St. Joseph's while Walters stayed home. He sat at the bar and watched the bubbles rise in a glass of beer he'd poured for Irvin. They'd have to wait for the ground to thaw before they could bury him.

⁂

BLACKJACK HAD LOST a visible amount of weight, and he looked altered, as if hibernation had been a kind of metamorphosis. When Walters went in to feed him, Blackjack acted petulant and huffed and pawed the ground and wouldn't let Walters get near. Walters filled Blackjack's bowl with dry cereal and a few leftover potato rolls, and then he scrammed. After Blackjack finished eating, he moved along the edge of the fencing, stopping to sometimes mark a spot with urine. For a while he took some interest in one of his old play sticks, until a drop of water fell on his head. He got up and stood on his hind legs, sniffing at the saturated canvas on top of the pen. Blackjack pawed at the spot, and then licked at it, and then just held his face there, letting the water pat him on the tip of his nose.

⁂

WALTERS FOUND A veterinarian in Rhinelander, a large-animal doctor named Dennis Urlinger who primarily dealt with horses and dairy cows. He wanted extra for the travel.

What Walters wanted was to have Blackjack's claws removed. He'd decided to see if it was possible after Blackjack grabbed hold of his jacket one day, reaching into the pocket for some of the sugar cubes Walters had been training him with. Blackjack kept digging deeper, trying to scoop out the sweets, and then his paw got caught. Blackjack started twisting and fighting with the coat, jerking Walters around, snapping him back and forth. The sudden panic made Walters think back to the time he caught his finger in a drill press, the quick snatching. Walters felt a claw poke through his clothes and into his side. Blackjack tore the pocket off Walters's jacket, spilling the sugar cubes onto the concrete. Walters tried kicking a few away, not wanting to reward Blackjack, but then Blackjack squared his lips at him and Walters let him have them all.

The veterinarian darted Blackjack with ketamine, a common horse tranquilizer. After Blackjack had fallen limp, the veterinarian followed Walters inside the pen, and the two men spread Blackjack out on his side. Walters squatted down by Blackjack's head, stroking his fur, waiting for the veterinarian to give him something to do. The vet was still getting out his tools. He had a pair of angle tongs, a pair of pliers, a tooth file, scissors, a scalpel, and a glazier's hammer.

"I don't know," he said, looking at the things he'd brought. He picked up one of Blackjack's paws, and it nearly filled his hand. "I hope they pluck right out."

Walters's job was to help hold. Each claw made a wet, cracking noise as it came loose, and the veterinarian made a pile of them in a bowl that Walters had brought out from the Stargazer. The vet swabbed each hole with iodine, going back a second time to the spots that kept bleeding.

"You're going to have to watch him," he said to Walters. "I don't think he's going to like this at first. But if they really keep bothering him, that might be an infection." The veterinarian checked Blackjack's eyes, pressed a stethoscope to his side, and then felt his nose. "We're done," he said, and started cleaning up his equipment.

Walters bent down and put an ear against Blackjack, right behind his left front leg, listening for a heartbeat. He heard something, something clear but coming from far away: *ta-dup, ta-dup.*

꿏

WALTERS HAD BEEN trying to teach Blackjack to waltz when they first started wrestling. Initially, it was mostly leaning and shoving and holding each other at arm's length. Blackjack weighed more than two hundred pounds by then, and on his hind legs stood a foot taller than Walters. When Walters shouldered into him, Blackjack felt as solid as a wall.

Walters's best defense was to keep one hand against Blackjack's throat, with the other arm pressed against the bear's chest. Sometimes instead of pushing and pulling on each other, the two just played their own miscued version of patty-cake.

As soon as Blackjack got his paws up around Walters's head that first time, Walters knew he was in trouble. Blackjack bent Walters's neck forward, and Walters had no choice but to obey. He could smell Blackjack's breath, could feel the hot huff against his ear. Before Walters had a chance to ready himself, he hit the ground with a thud. The pain flashed white, cracked right through him.

He sensed the bear above. His wind had been knocked out, and Walters struggled to take in a breath. His ribs were bruised. He imagined Blackjack standing on his hind legs, about to slam those paws down on his back, a blow to stun him before he split him open as easily as a pumpkin. Walters wanted to scream, but nothing seemed to come out.

"No, Blackjack," he finally said, raspy. "Enough." The bear only sniffed Walters's skull, upset and worried.

§

WHEN THE BENCHES filled, people stood in the aisles. Others stood on overturned milk crates, or they climbed aboard Walters's boats, or they hung from trees. It had taken Walters over a month to build the ring and the seating and to find a suitable bell. Walters promised Irvin Klomatski's younger brother, who was seventy years old himself, five bucks if he stood at the entrance and collected the admission fee. The night was billed as Man vs. Bear, a quarter per person. It was to be a one-time-only event, though Walters already had plans to make it a weekly summertime occurrence—every Saturday night at the Stargazer.

A few people in the crowd were tourists, unsure of themselves, but most of the spectators were locals, and many hoped Walters would be eaten alive. Walters had asked Dennis Urlinger to be the referee in trade for a small percentage of the door, but he declined and instead gave Walters the phone number for his brother-in-law, who needed the money. Tooty's job was to make sure nobody stole any drinks.

Mike sat in the third row with his wife, Alice. The Schumachers were there. The Dietzen brothers. The Jootsens. Katy Strohm. Boyd Randerson. Glenn Holzknecht. Walters had grudged with every one of them at some point, had run everyone's patience dry. Even Tooty, somewhere inside her, felt Walters had something coming, and that maybe this would be his time.

"I didn't expect this," Mike said to Alice. A canopy of light strings shone above him. He noted the megaphone sitting in a corner of the ring.

"No," Alice said. "This is beyond." Whatever was going to happen next, this was already something.

Blackjack made his entrance first, led on his leash by the referee.

"Jesus," Mike caught himself saying, inching closer to Alice. Along with almost everyone else they cheered and clapped and whistled, doubly so when Blackjack stood on his hind legs and yawned, which many thought was a growl. When Walters entered the ring, some continued to applaud, while others began to jeer him. A scoop of ice cream flew his way.

"Good luck!" someone yelled, while Walters waved off the crowd. People booed.

"Boooo," Mike joined in, quiet enough that only Alice could hear. When he got her to smile, she elbowed him in the side and told him to quit it.

The referee brought Walters and Blackjack together in the center of the ring, gave them the rules and told them to shake, which they did. Alice found it funny. Mike wasn't sure, and he had the urge to keep booing.

When the bell rang, Walters and Blackjack locked together. It was the same game they had been playing for months now, something that had finally become a dance. They leaned into each other, pushing back and forth. Walters held his forearm against Blackjack's chest, keeping him back, and when the crowd grew disappointed that Blackjack wasn't winning, Walters played it up and tried to look bored.

"Break it up," someone in the crowd yelled to the referee, who didn't think he was actually supposed to officiate.

Walters and Blackjack squared off again, and this time Walters signaled Blackjack to come put his paws on his shoulders. Walters squirmed and grimaced and made it look as if Blackjack had him. This is what they wanted to see. Walters, having to conceal his smile, pushed his face into Blackjack's hide and began tickling him. "Hug," he said, so that Blackjack would wrap his wide arms around him.

Walters stood on his tiptoes to make it seem like Blackjack was lifting him off the ground, as if he was about to be squeezed in half. Walters's arms were pinned, and each breath looked more labored than the next. When Walters's head lolled, a woman in the crowd gasped.

At the right time, Walters would tell Blackjack to release him. Blackjack would drop him to the mat, and then Walters would get up and go two more rounds before the part where Blackjack let Walters pin him. The referee would slap the mat, and the crowd would moan.

But now the choreography called for Walters to shriek as if he was in terrible anguish. Many hoped it was true. Mike leaned forward on his seat. While some thought he was dying, while some smiled at this possibility, and a few felt sick to their stomachs, Walters rubbed Blackjack's favorite spot and whispered for him to hold tighter.

"Good boy," he praised. "Good boy."

THERE WAS A constant flickering of light and shadow as the train passed through the woodlands. Even with his eyes closed, Walters noticed it. Like Morse code, the intervals of light and shade seemed to be made of dots and dashes, tapping in and out of synchronicity with the sound of the train wheels hitting the joints in the track. He'd eaten a big lunch and was sleepy, and the backs of his eyelids made a kind of movie screen, one where the voices of passengers blurred together. Far down the train, in his very own baggage car, Blackjack was chained to the floor of his cage.

In the seat behind Walters, a young boy and girl—a brother and sister, Walters guessed—were talking about what they thought the ocean would look like.

"Like a lake," the boy said, "but it'll be so big you can't see the other side."

"I think it'll be bigger than that," the girl said. "I think it'll look like the sky."

Walters thought that maybe they were equally right. Once he'd been out on Lake Michigan and had lost sight of the shore, and for a moment he felt as if he was just a figurine trapped inside a giant glass ball. He guessed maybe the ocean would be something like that.

"And there'll be sharks," the boy said. "And whales, and dolphins, and fish that can sting you."

Walters wondered if his boats were still sitting behind the tavern. It all belonged to someone else now. He wondered if Tooty was still at her sister's.

"There aren't," the girl said.

"There are."

Your brother is right, Walters thought. There'll be all sorts of things you've never seen. Palm trees. Mansions. Bikini girls. He wanted to ask them if they'd ever seen a bear ride a bicycle. He should have told them they'd see plenty of the old things too.

Suddenly the light stopped flickering, and Walters knew they had passed into a clearing. "Look," he heard the girl say.

"Oh," is all her brother said. "Wow."

Walters guessed cows. He was still swirling with images of palm trees and movie lots and television studios—they were headed for Blackjack's first job, an episode of *Lassie* titled "The Bear"—and he thought the train was probably just crossing some pastures. That's all this place was good for, the production of manure.

"Is that it?" the girl asked. "Are we at the ocean?"

"No," her brother said. "That's the Mississippi."

When Walters opened his eyes, he couldn't believe the size of the river. The train was not even a quarter of the way across the channel.

"Look," the boy said. Walters started scanning for something, as if the kid had been talking to him. "Look, that's a barge. They weigh thousands of pounds but they still float!" The boy hadn't believed it was possible.

Walters turned and leaned over his seat back. The boy and girl were both pressed close to the window—the girl in her seat, the boy standing. "See the towboats," Walters said gently. "The smaller ones, those are the towboats."

"Yes," the boy said. He had read books all about them. "They push instead of pull."

"Is that so?" Walters asked, though he knew the kid was exactly right.

"Oh, my gosh," the boy said, holding his head in his hands. "This is the best moment of my life."

The best moment, Walters thought, so far.

Close is Fine

I WAS ON my way home from Gerald's when I decided to detour past the Evergreen and see if Kirsten was still working. Friday nights were busy, and I knew I'd probably have to sit at the bar, that anything I wanted to say to her would have to fit into bits of conversation that lasted no longer than what it took for her to load her drink tray. We'd agreed on the divorce months ago, but Kirsten and I were still living in the same house, sleeping in separate bedrooms, waiting for the final splintering to happen. I didn't know what I was going to say to Kirsten, but for some reason, I thought there was something I could say. Something that could return us to the lives we used to live.

We'd been good about staying out of each other's way. I was working for Dale Pismire then, so I was gone early each dawn, and I was rarely back before Kirsten left for the Evergreen. Kirsten usually came home around two in the morning, long after I'd gone to bed. The noise of her entering the house often woke me, and sometimes I'd lie in the dark listening to her moving around downstairs—the keys hitting the table, a faucet running—trying hard not to think about how scared I could get. Some nights I was too groggy to think very much, and I fell right back into a heavy, workman's rest. Other times, I was up until sunrise, which is not when the birds start chirping, but when they finally shut up.

I considered turning around, but I kept driving—the windows open, the warm air swirling like a tornado inside my shitty little Dodge Colt.

I had cash in my pocket. I'd drunk enough beers at Gerald's to think I needed more.

All summer, Gerald had been working on a nearly life-sized replica of an MI98 Howitzer, this massive piece of artillery he'd seen on some Discovery Channel show about Afghanistan. He'd recorded the program on his VCR, and he'd pause the tape and use the static-ruined still frames to get a better idea of all the parts. He was making the thing mostly out of scrap wood, and it didn't even have a hollow barrel, but Gerald was going to drag it out to the end of his driveway and drape an American flag from it and let it be some kind of reminder for what was really at stake.

Sometimes I'd go over and hold the end of the tape measure for Gerald, or help him feed a sheet of wood through his table saw, but otherwise I kept to the sidelines. The Howitzer was his deal, and I was fine just watching. Being with Gerald sometimes made me think of being a teenager again, when my dad would drag me out to the garage to help him change the oil in the car, or to work on some repair. Then he'd just expect me to hold the light for him, or pass him the socket wrench, to be like some sponge and sit there and soak up all his wisdom. At Gerald's place I often just watched and listened to him explain what he was doing, and then let it all bounce right off me. I answered with things like, "Gotcha," or, "That's slick," because I knew that's what he wanted to hear, and it didn't make any sense to point out all the ways he should've been doing it different, not for something I had no stake in.

By the time I got to the Evergreen, I felt wrung out. When I didn't see Kirsten's car in the parking lot, I decided to leave. I could feel the sweat dried to my eyebrows, could feel it, like some kind of shellac, covering the back of my neck. A shower suddenly sounded better than a beer. My tool belt was sitting on the passenger-side floor, where Gerald had moved it when I'd given him a ride home. I wondered if Kirsten had finished her shift early, and for a fleeting moment I pictured her in our kitchen—the kitchen she had always wanted—heating up leftovers and setting out plates for the both of us. It was twenty miles of flat, pine-hedged highway until I got there.

ONE OF THE reasons Kirsten and I still lived together was our house. With Gerald's help, and a few subcontractors from Antigo, and with a lot of work from Kirsten actually, I'd built that whole thing from a modified garage blueprint. It was a simple, gambrel-roofed design. One-and-a-half baths and a loft space, which had recently become my bedroom. The building was sound, and everything had passed the major inspections, but in the year that Kirsten and I had been living in it, I hadn't completed any of the finish work. I still hadn't put up most of the trim or finished the caulking, hadn't put the doors on the cabinets in the laundry room, hadn't finished the top course of siding. They were all little things, I thought, things that I had really stopped seeing. Things that were nothing more extraordinary than the dirty dishes, or the laundry, or any of the other untidy things in life that I could never seem to get caught up with.

But Kirsten could keep up. She did get the laundry folded, and the dishes put away, and the bills paid early. It bothered her to leave things unfinished, or at least unfinished for very long. In the spring, when it was time to take the storm windows off and I didn't help her, she gave me an ultimatum. I could either finish the work on the house, or she was going to do it herself. I tried explaining to her that she didn't know how to cut an inside joint, and that she still hadn't ever used the nail gun because she was afraid of it. When I told her that it'd look ugly if she did it, that it'd lower the selling price more than if we just left it unfinished, Kirsten gave me her revision.

"You have a couple options," she said. If I didn't finish the work by fall, we'd put it on the market as is and hope we could get enough out of it. "Or you can buy me out," she said, knowing full well that I didn't have the means. "My father," she went on, as if I hadn't already heard what she was about to say a million times from my own dad, "he always told me that if you were going to do something, you should do it right, or that you shouldn't do it at all." She had a handkerchief tied around her head, and wore one of my old flannels, had on a pair of jeans with ripped knees. She had a bottle of Windex in one hand, a crumpled-up sheet of newspaper in the other. Her lips had disappeared—her mouth was only a thin, straight line. "In the future," she said, "I think you should be more of the not-at-all type."

❦

I TURNED OFF the highway and onto Deerbrook, the gravel road that Kirsten and I shared with a few mobile homes and hunting shacks. The washboards had grown unavoidable, even when drifting from one side of the road to the other, and the car vibrated horribly, right up through my teeth. My tools tinked against themselves, and I thought that I'd probably leave them right where they were all weekend.

I'd gotten a few things done since the ultimatum—I'd finished putting the handles and strike plates on all the doors, patched and painted the spot on the bathroom ceiling where I'd cut the hole for the exhaust vent too big—enough to make it look like I was trying. Because I was. I had put a lot into the house already. And I didn't want Kirsten to be right about me. There were two-by-fours in the walls that had my blood on them. Some of the job had been sloppy, like the bathroom, but with other parts, like the molding around the fireplace, and the tiling and the countertops in the kitchen, I'd done work I was happy with. Despite what had happened to my marriage, I was proud of the house, and I wanted to see it completed, though I also knew that would mean the end of everything else.

I stopped at the end of the driveway to check the mailbox. A *Super Shopper* was the only piece waiting for me, so I left it there and put up the flag, hoping I could just send it back. Kirsten wasn't home. When I saw the empty parking spot, I knew she was on a date. I don't know how I knew, except that I suddenly felt something stone-like in my gut. I sat in my car a while, listening to the engine clicking as it cooled, and I stared at the shafts of light seeping through the woods around the house. I had the same stirred-up feeling as when I watched porn. My blood felt thinned out, my hands shaky. The forest seemed so claustrophobic. Whoever she was with would call me a fool for letting her go. And he'd be right, except I didn't let go. I was more of a pusher-awayer.

❦

THE DAY I told Kirsten I'd slept with another woman, we'd gone to Antigo to rent a U-Haul for the move. But the truck they were going to rent us wouldn't start, and we sat there for forty-five minutes while they tried jumping it. Then they switched out the battery, though I could hear right away that the problem was with the solenoid, and the engine never did turn over. I tried giving them a hand, but the manager had his own ideas and wouldn't listen, so I let the jackass flounder.

"Help him," Kirsten kept saying to me.

"I can't," I said.

Kirsten and I had already moved a few things to the house, but the U-Haul was supposed to be our big move, where we'd empty out one place and fill the other in a single trip. Kirsten had been excited, and each time the truck didn't start, a little bit of her energy washed away. The U-Haul place also rented tools and banquet tables, and it only had one other truck, which was already reserved.

"Otherwise, I'd give it to you," the manager said, when Kirsten tried pouting. "How about a trailer?" he asked. His polo shirt had slid up his round gut a wink, and with all that insulation he was sweating a good bit. His hands were blackened with grease, and he wiped at them with a faded pink rag. "Can't do anything about a truck until tomorrow."

We were on our way home when I told Kirsten. I thought honesty was more important than not being a dick. The girl's name was Heidi Sprister, and she was only twenty-three years old—twelve years younger than me—though I didn't tell Kirsten any of that.

"I'm not necessarily surprised," Kirsten said. She spoke softly and seemed calm, and for a moment I started to smile, because I thought maybe it could be that painless.

We were passing an old, beat-to-shit farmhouse that we'd passed a million times, one that had bits of junk scattered all around it, even way out in the fields where the cows were grazing. Kirsten's attention seemed to be taken by the scene. On my side of the road, it was all corn. When I looked back, Kirsten's shoulders were heaving, and I thought she was crying.

"Hey," I said, touching her on the forearm.

Kirsten laughed—a sort of exasperated, disbelieving huff. She hadn't been crying at all. "That's just great," she said, turning to me. "Great fucking job, Tanner. Congratulations on becoming an asshole."

We didn't say anything the rest of the way home. I tried not to think of Heidi. The car felt so small, I thought Kirsten was sure to read my thoughts. We'd been married for two years, and I think I knew that it was over then, or that it would be over, that it wouldn't last another two, though ultimately it did.

I kept thinking of reasons I wasn't an asshole, and reasons Kirsten was, though none of the evidence seemed very solid.

"Here," I said, once we got home. Kirsten had gotten out of the car, and I held out the pamphlet for the U-Haul, which had our receipt for the truck inside. "We can't lose this," I said.

"What are you doing?" she asked, shutting her door. She looked as tired as I'd ever seen her, and as bored.

I didn't know if she meant at that moment, or in general. In general, I had no idea. "I'm going to go work on the house," I said. "I want to at least get something done today." I spent the afternoon just firing the nail gun into the woods, hoping each time I pulled the trigger that I'd finally have a real answer for her.

❧

IT WAS THREE in the morning when I woke up, an hour past last call. I listened for Kirsten, but the house was quiet. Any second, I thought, she'd walk through that door. Any second. Any second. Any second.

I knew she wasn't home, but I went downstairs anyway to see. Her car was still gone, and I stood looking out into the driveway, the pole light I left on for her humming like some insect. I went around the house turning on even more lights. I moved through the kitchen, into the living room, down the hallway, the laundry room, right up to her bedroom, which I'd been peeking into for weeks.

. All the old furniture was still there—our bed, a dresser my grandmother had handed down to Kirsten, the little end table I'd pieced together from old barn boards. She'd moved things around, and taken the pictures off the wall, but I recognized everything. A pair of her jeans hung on the end of the bed, which was still unmade. A stack of folded laundry sat in the chair. A few pairs of underwear, just some old everyday ones, grey with blue and green stripes, were right on top. We had stopped doing each other's laundry a long time ago, and I went and lifted up the panties and tried to imagine the shape they would take on her. Kirsten was small, almost bony. In the winter her chest was so pale that blue veins showed through. Toward the end, I associated her size with a kind of frailty. But now I remember that her size was the thing I always loved, that I felt so big when I wrapped her in my arms.

❧

HEIDI AND I met at an old fishing lodge called the Wolf River Inn, which was run by a white-haired spitfire named Joan Jenske. I'd been having trouble piecing together enough work that year, and I'd taken on a job doing maintenance for Joan twice a week. The Inn had been built in the twenties, and everything seemed to be held together by a series of bad patch jobs. The rooms were damp, and smelled moldy if they got closed up for too long. I tried talking Joan into letting me gut a couple and redo them right, but for Joan, patches had to do.

Heidi worked as the housekeeper, and I always saw her ferrying laundry between the cabins and the main lodge, zipping around in Joan's sun-bleached golf cart. Once I even saw her spinning donuts with it.

I had been fixing the thermostat in Cabin Four when Heidi came in to clean. "Hey," she said, chomping on a piece of gum. She was pushing a vacuum cleaner in front of her, dragging a mesh bag full of towels behind, and she had to slow down to navigate her way around my toolbox. "You're okay," she said, when I tried sliding it out of the way.

Heidi was curvy and full and wore tight-fitting Wranglers. I imagined that she'd probably been a terror on her high school softball team, though I never asked her if that was true. She had long, sandy hair that she most often wore pulled back in a ponytail, or pulled through the back of a ball cap. She'd only started working at the Inn since her husband had been called to Iraq. It was Darren's second tour, 32nd Infantry Brigade, Red Arrow Division. Otherwise he worked for the highway department building roads.

"By the end of the summer," she once said to me, snapping out a top sheet and letting it drift down to the bed, "I swear he's browner than a Mexican."

Some of the fishermen that came to Joan's liked to have a good time. They weren't scary rowdy, like some of the biker bars around here, but the rowdy that was suburban men letting loose—*SportsCenter*, too much alcohol, a few dirty jokes. They were the kind of guys who knew enough of work that they'd see me patching something and come over and shoot the shit, and get in my way, and offer me beers, and tell me how sweet they thought my life in paradise must be. They'd ask me where the good fishing was when they should have been asking Joan, who'd fished the river all her life. Most of them didn't even really care, would only cast a couple flies in the hottest part of the day, quit, and then start celebrating.

Sometimes they invited me to their parties. I was trudging past a cabin one day when a group of guys from Madison asked me to join them. I'd been weed-whacking for hours, and I just wanted to put that damn trimmer away.

"We're trying to have a barbeque here," a guy said, holding up his half-eaten bratwurst. "And you're working too hard for us to have any fun."

"Just keeping my boss happy," I said. I was sunburned, had gotten stung by a wasp, and my pants were stained green up to the knees.

"Come on," the guy said. The grill smelled good, like grease and charcoal. "Hamburgers, hot dogs, whatever you want."

I hadn't seen Heidi at first. She was sitting on the deck, her back against the wall, an empty paper plate in her lap. Everyone else was standing, or sitting up on the deck railing, which I was always having to fix because of people always sitting on it. When Heidi noticed me, she gave a little half-wave. She raised the red plastic cup she'd been drinking from, and then shrugged her shoulders.

"Okay," I said, thirsty as hell. "Let me clock out."

The group was more my age than Heidi's, the kind of guys who sported pleated pants and had nice watches and wore visors with the Titleist logo on them. They'd made some kind of punch, some mixture of alcohol and fruit juice that was too sweet and too poisonous and left a drink mustache. By the time I'd started in on my burger, I was already spinning.

Heidi had spent the day cleaning rooms, and I could smell the bleach, even though I was pretty ripe myself. Sometimes Heidi found the cabins trashed. By the way these guys were going, Joan's dog would be licking their puke out of the bushes in the morning.

"Want me to drop a hint about not leaving you too big a mess?" I asked.

Heidi nibbled on the rim of her cup. "Just tell them to not leave any wadded-up, crusty towels."

"Really?" I asked.

"You don't even know," she said.

I told her I didn't believe it, though I knew it was probably true.

"Help sometime," she said, "and you can see for yourself."

After it got dark, the party moved off the deck and over to the fire pit, which was centered between all the cabins. I told the guys where the woodpile was, told them to help themselves, but they'd packed the trunks of their cars full of firewood, and they didn't want to have to haul it back home. There were several wooden chairs around the fire pit. A few notched-out logs, the kind of big logs you couldn't find around here anymore, served as benches. Heidi and I huddled together on one of them. The air was damp and cool, and the river burbled in the background. It felt nice, having our shoulders touch, and for the first time in a long time, I seemed to remember that I was a living, breathing person who could steer his own life in whatever direction he wanted.

Heidi and I didn't talk much, but we stayed like that, leaning into one another. I watched the sparks dance off the fire, watched the white-hot center of the pit, all the while trying to silently will one of Heidi's arms around me. The guys told stories based on stories they all already knew. One of them had a guitar out, though he couldn't play any songs. I think Heidi and I were the only two listening to him.

She said sure when I asked her if she wanted to go for a walk. There weren't any streetlights out past the Inn's driveway. It was colder away from the fire, and there wasn't anywhere to go really, but we could still hear the guys laughing it up, and we kept walking. We could hardly see the road. We walked all the way to Steed's Landing, our strides lengthening as we went downhill. At the end of the road, I started running, my hands straight out in front of me for protection.

We had sex that night on the picnic table at the landing. There wasn't much current at Steed's, but the river still swirled and gurgled as it bent around all the rocks. The water looked as if it was made of ink. It was the first and only time I've ever had sex outside, under the stars, and it was uncontrolled and multi-positioned and fun—everything that sex with Kirsten was not—though it was also burdened by the feeling that I was performing some kind of demolition on my life, the same kind of sledge-hammer gutting I'd been pressing Joan to do with her rooms.

The next two weeks, while Kirsten was at the Evergreen and Darren was trying not to get IED'd by some towel head, I drove over to Heidi's to steal away a couple of hours. Sometimes she did a whole striptease for me, right there in the living room, the TV glowing behind her. She and Darren lived in a newish double-wide on a quarter-acre lot, and there were reminders of him all through the place. Heidi and I didn't talk about our other halves, but at times I couldn't stop thinking of Kirsten, and at other times—like when I once pulled out and turned Heidi over, and she responded by telling me to show her how strong I was—I thought of Darren, way out in the middle of hell. There was a portrait of him in his dress blues out in the hallway. Sometimes I'd stop and look at it, try-ing to pretend he was from another world, from some other dimension where this kind of thing was cool. Where these things had no effect on the future, and sent no ripples.

☙

KIRSTEN DIDN'T COME home until late the next afternoon, with just enough time to take a shower and eat before she had to leave for work. I was outside putting my tools away when her car pulled into the driveway. I looked up briefly, then put my head back down to make it seem like I didn't care, or that I couldn't be bothered, though my heart felt like it was trying to punch its way out my chest. I'd finished the shingling, and had put the screens on the soffit vents. I'd even worked on knocking down the pile of dirt in the yard, so we could finally get a lawn. The only way I could function was to keep my hands busy, and keep my mind focused on other things, like the addition of fractions, or making sure that I followed a straight line.

"Looks nice," Kirsten said. She'd come over to the scrap pile and stood there with her arms folded across her chest, her purse hanging from the crook of an elbow. Her white dress shirt and bra were slung over her shoulder.

"Yeah," I said, and got busy picking up the cuts.

Kirsten squatted down, careful to make sure her purse didn't go into the dirt, and she picked up a little triangle of cedar by the corner, holding it between her thumb and forefinger, as if it was a used tissue or something, and she tossed it into the Rubbermaid bucket. She picked up three or four pieces that way. When she stood up, her sunglasses slid off the top of her head and back onto her face.

"I hope you didn't worry," she said, putting the glasses in her purse.

"I tried not to," I said. "I was a little. I figured you were okay." I hadn't really been worried. That's not what it was.

Kirsten stood over me, watching me toss the last of the pieces in the bucket. How many of these buckets had I already filled in my life? Her nipples were pressing through her tank top, and I kept looking up at them. Off in the distance, I could hear someone running a chainsaw. I tried to think of everything I'd finished that day, tried to be content with one thing at a time. I thought that's how things were built: by increments, by little pieces, nailed together in a way that could keep out the cold.

Kirsten said she had to get ready for work. "What else do you have to get ready for?" I blurted out, just as she turned to go inside.

Kirsten frowned at me and asked if I wanted to explain that one some more.

"Can you please come home tonight?" I said.

"I probably won't," she said. "I already have plans. Sorry."

I wanted to know what plans.

"It doesn't matter," she said. "They're plans."

Then I asked her if he had a big dick. It's embarrassing to say I was so childish. That I would ask the one question I didn't really want to know the answer to, when there were so many others I really did want answered, like what would happen if we tried again.

"Use your imagination," she said, and held her hands at least two feet apart.

❦

AFTER KIRSTEN LEFT for work, I couldn't stand being in the house alone, so I drove out to Gerald's. He was in his kitchen putting together a tuna melt when I came over. "Want one?" he asked, unwrapping a cheese single.

If I hadn't had to drive him around, I'm not sure I would have ever become friends with Gerald. I never had anything against him, but I wasn't much into making friends those days, even with the guys I worked with. He'd had his license revoked after his third DUI in two years. He even spent a few weeks in jail. When he came to work for Dale, and when he kept showing up late because he was always hitchhiking, Dale made me pick Gerald up each morning and make sure he got to the job site on time. Dale said Gerald could find his own way home, and that I shouldn't feel obliged, and maybe I didn't, but I gave him a ride home every night, or I at least dropped him off part way. I took him grocery shopping, drove him into town so he could buy a bigger TV when the Packers were making another run at it. Once I even took him all the way down to Appleton to visit his grandmother.

I don't know if Gerald gave good suggestions, but he always had a lot of them, and though I usually never took his advice, I liked the fact that there was always plenty to sift through. We were the same age, and he was a pretty fun guy to be around, even though he was always listening to talk radio. He'd never been married, but he'd lived with a few girls over the years, and was even engaged once, which he thought made him know a thing or three about women. He talked moves, saw going to the bar as a kind of sport. He liked to brag about his bachelor life, though sometimes he'd tell me how he wished he were in my shoes—married, even if it was heading for divorce—and I could tell he was thinking about Lorie, his almost-wife.

We ate on Gerald's back porch and watched the sun pull the day over the horizon, the sky shifting from a blaze of yellow and orange to gray and then black. Gerald knew that I'd slept with Heidi, knew that she was also married, but not that her husband was part of the Army National Guard. The way Gerald saw it, or so he told me many times, my affair with Heidi was totally understandable. He said he probably would have done the same thing, and probably sooner than I had. But I knew he didn't know the whole story, and that if he knew about Darren he wouldn't have felt the same way. Once when some Marine called in to one of Gerald's radio shows and told a story about his wife cheating on him while he was off in Fallujah, Gerald called it treason.

"This guy is protecting our freedom, and then this other guy is banging his wife as thanks. People like that should be shot in the balls," Gerald said. "Fallujah," he added a second later, shaking his head as if the word held wonder. "Fucking Fal-lu-jah."

Gerald had staged the Howitzer next to the garage. When the sky got dark enough, the automated outdoor lights kicked on, illuminating one side of that monster and throwing a silhouette across the yard. Gerald had made a lot of progress since Friday night. He'd been concentrating on the Howitzer's breech end, where he'd added three different hand wheels, though his wheels were actually square. Each of the wheels spun smoothly, though they didn't have any effect on the up-and-down or side-to-side of the barrel, like they would've on a real one.

"How do you like that?" Gerald asked me, as I tested one of the wheels. The barrel was fixed at a forty-five degree angle. He picked up my plate from the porch and stacked it on his, and then drained the last of his soda. He'd been doing pretty well with not drinking alcohol.

"I like it," I said, seeing that he looked pretty proud. "They spin."

"That's what I mean," he said.

Gerald had rounded off the corners of a two-by-two to make what I knew was the telescope. I found it leaning against the carriage. While Gerald was in the kitchen, I held up the telescope and tried to see how it'd fit, wondering exactly where it went. As I did, I thought of Gerald, and how he'd probably done the same thing all afternoon, holding up the pieces to see how they'd match, or how he could make them work.

"What's with this?" I asked when he came back. I cocked back the wood like I was going to smash a fastball into the night.

"I don't know," Gerald said. "I have to figure out how I want to build the mount up." He took the telescope from me and showed me where it would go. "There'll be an elbow here," he said. "That's how they really are. So you can just look in like this." He stepped forward, as if he was about to look through the scope and check the coordinates, see where his armaments would fall.

For a while Gerald and I tinkered around in his shop, spreading out a pile of hardware on the workbench and seeing if anything might work for the telescope mount. The fluorescent lights in the shop drew in a bunch of moths, and they beat themselves against the bulbs. There was a dusty, oily smell that reminded me of the interior of my grandfather's truck. Rather than looking for a piece to attach the telescope with, Gerald seemed more interested in just going through all the brackets and hangers and split pins and trying to remember where all the stuff had even come from. Something had gotten in me, and instead of sitting back, I really wanted to build a piece of the Howitzer, wanted to get the telescope mounted and be able to stand back and look and be satisfied that I'd done well. "What about this?" I asked him, about a galvanized U-bracket.

Gerald was playing with an old cow magnet, seeing how many things he could pick up at once before the string of metal broke.

"Hmmm," he said, as if he hadn't heard. "Maybe." I held the bracket out so he could see it better. He took the bracket from me and tested it with the magnet, the two pieces snapping together.

"I'm not sure what I want to do exactly," he said. "I'm thinking of cutting a couple four-by-sixes down, and making a whole sort of mounting block. I have a vision. But not a plan."

I waited for him to give the piece back, because I wanted to see if it'd work, but he just tossed it back in the pile.

"Do you think they can feel that inside them?" I asked about the magnet. "Do you think they know?"

"I wonder," Gerald said. "If they eat all that metal in the first place. Maybe not."

"What if there was a magnet you could put in your head?" I asked. "One that attracted all your bad ideas together in a quiet corner, so they couldn't move around and cause trouble?"

"You'd probably feel that," he said.

GERALD AND I drove up toward Post Lake, not far from where we'd been working for Dale. There were a lot of back roads up there that we'd never been on, and we followed them along, randomly turning right and left at each stop sign, wondering if we'd eventually come to some place we recognized. It was past midnight, the roads empty. Gerald and I had a few cans of beer with us, and I drove with an open one resting between my legs. I had the radio tuned to the country station, but the volume turned low. The roads dipped and curved, and we kept coming upon all these small kettle lakes that had no public access because they were ringed with cottages. A pair of blue reflectors marked every driveway. Almost all the houses were dark, except for a few porch lights.

"You shouldn't be able to own a lake," Gerald said. "Unless you dig it yourself."

We climbed away from the water, up onto some flatlands, where the potato fields started to take over. Deer stood far enough back to miss the brush of the headlights, but I could see their dark outlines along the roadside. Many times they didn't even look up as we passed, but when they did, and if they turned their heads just the right way, their eyes caught enough light and glowed pale blue like little moons.

"Slow down," Gerald said, motioning in the same way you'd tell a backhoe to keep lowering its bucket. "Way down."

We crept along until we came to the next group of deer—what I thought were three does. I eased forward, bringing the car to a stop about thirty yards away, parking so that the headlights shined directly on them. Two of the deer stopped eating and lifted their heads and stared back at Gerald and me. Their big ears twitched and flicked like a horse's.

When he took a few steps toward the road, I saw then that the third deer was actually a little spiked buck. "See that?" I asked. His antlers were still covered in felt. It meant they were soft, and still growing.

I kept the deer centered in the high beams. I don't know how many hundreds of deer I've seen in my life, but as we shined them that night the deer seemed new to me, as familiar but as odd as a newborn child must seem to its parents. The deer had traversed the ditch and were climbing the embankment onto the road. The buck had stepped in front, and he stood between the two girls and us. He was a pretty scrawny thing, and I wondered how long he'd make it, if he'd survive until his splay of antlers had grown to ten, twelve, fourteen points.

The deer seemed so exposed as they lingered on the road. "Should we shoo them?" I wondered.

"If a car starts coming," Gerald said. "Then we should honk or something."

As we waited for the deer to make it across the road, I told Gerald about Kirsten. Speculated that she was probably with the dude right then. I said, "My mind just races."

"Man," Gerald said. Way down the road, a pair of headlights appeared out of the dark. The deer were almost to the other side. "Well, that sucks," he said. "She couldn't wait?"

"I didn't."

"It resets after that. It starts from there."

What was Kirsten supposed to wait for? How often had I told her that she should find some guy, even if I'd meant it mostly sarcastically?

"I don't know," I said to Gerald, wanting to defend Kirsten. "That seems arbitrary." I could see the part in me that was supposed to be happy for her, could see it sitting there in front of me, as clear as a glass of water.

"Maybe this is a good thing," he said. "You know? Now it's your turn. Find some girl to go stay the night with. Hook up. Get laid. Be well."

The headlights grew larger, and the deer hesitated on the opposite shoulder of the road. I tapped the horn, and revved my car's toy engine. "I mean, I can show you," Gerald said. "I can show you how it's done. But then you're going to have to take it from there."

I hit the horn again, scattering the deer. "You're right," I said, because I knew Gerald wouldn't understand if I told him how ridiculous he sounded to me. I was thinking something more in line with a monastery, or jamming a screwdriver in my neck. "That's a good idea," I said. "Get on with things, right?"

"Lock and load," Gerald said. "That's exactly right."

THAT FIRST NIGHT she didn't come home, the night that I padded downstairs and went and held a pair of her underwear, and then stayed up watching infomercials, and then went outside and stood in the backyard and stared at the marbled black sky, hoping a star would break loose so that I could wish everything better, I went back to Kirsten's room and looked through her stuff. I found her diary in the drawer next to the bed. It was just a plain old Mead notebook, and I'd only ever seen her write in it a handful of times, but when I flipped through, almost all the pages were full.

There was a list of New Year's promises from all the way back in 2000, when we were sure the world was going to end. She finished that entry with a *dot dot dot*.

There was a sketch of how she wanted to landscape the backyard. We'd talked about a spot for a hammock, and a little fenced area where she could have roses the deer couldn't get. She wrote about things she'd been thinking lately—wondering how much it'd cost to take credit classes at the extension in Antigo, and if she might be able to trade in her car for something less rusty once the house sold. I don't know what I was looking for. I could tell by the frilly edge left in the spirals that a few pages had been torn out. I had to think those were the pages about me.

Then I read about Mark, the guy Kirsten had already slept with twice. In loopy cursive Kirsten wrote about the first time she'd waited on his table, how wide his smile was, the ten dollar tip. He'd come back a second time, and then a third, and finally she let him buy her some drinks. Later they drove a big square of highway, stopping at every little tavern along the way, dancing wherever they could. Eventually they wound up right back at the Evergreen so Kirsten could get her car. He followed her down the road to the Sleepy Inn, a little six-room hotel on the border of the reservation.

She wrote about the sex. How much she liked it when he had a finger up her and was sucking on her tits. She described the weight of him pushing down, her head getting pushed into the headboard. He'd told her how good she felt, how tight.

She'd had a fun time, but it was weird. She wanted to do it again. And so there was a second time, at our place, a lunch date. I hadn't come home for lunch ever since starting with Dale, but just in case, Kirsten locked the doors.

The details from that encounter were brief. Second time, she wrote, and no condom. *What the hell are you doing, Sikora?* It was her maiden name, underlined twice. She was almost a week late.

※

AFTER SHINING THE deer, Gerald and I drove to the jobsite to steal some wood—two-by-fours, mostly, some trim pieces, a couple of sheets of bead board. A chain and padlock spanned the driveway, which was a two-track through the grass, but both of us had keys. We'd been working at the site since March, except for a few weeks when Dale sent us off to build a garden shed for a woman who never went outside without putting on a wide-brimmed hat.

Before we started loading the wood, Gerald and I wandered out onto the back deck. We'd been at the house so often it felt like it was ours. All around us the tree frogs were talking. The lake looked purple, and out in the distance we could see the black lump of the small island, which you weren't supposed to go to because of a pair of loons nesting there. The lake house was the biggest project Dale had ever done, and though it was a beautiful piece of property—the lot had twelve hundred feet of waterfront—the whole thing had been a killer. From the road, the land sloped hard to the lake, and it was a horrible slant to work on. We put in the deck and a row of big windows to show off the lake, but until we got the foundation poured and the floors laid, we spent all day hobbling around on the side of a muddy hill. With just a little bit of rain, that clay turned slick as snot. The mosquitoes swarmed. It took two people to move a wheelbarrow—one pulling, one pushing—and all of us, even Dale, fell on our ass at some point. All the fixtures and cabinets and sinks and countertops were from specialty places, not the kinds of things you could just go into Antigo and get at the Fleet Farm, which is how Dale had mostly been doing it. We were constantly getting the wrong pieces— wrong color, wrong style—and sometimes we even installed them, only to take them out and ship them back and wait on their replacements.

"Do you think you could live here?" I asked Gerald.

"Here?" he asked. I could hear the water lapping against the shore. "Are you kidding me? Sitting in the lap of luxury, enjoying my view. I don't think it'd be a problem."

I didn't think he was lying, but I didn't believe him. The view was something, and the bathroom had a whirlpool tub, and the kitchen had granite countertops and an oversized, restaurant-quality stove, and even while there was still sawdust and sheets of clear plastic everywhere—even though the walls were unpainted, and uncapped pieces of Romex jutted out from several junction boxes—you could still see that it was the kind of place that made it into lifestyle magazines and onto TV shows, the kind of place that wasn't for people like Gerald and me, even though we'd built the thing.

"I don't know, man." Maybe for a few days, I thought. I'm sure Gerald pictured it being like some rap video, and that there'd be women in bikinis, and that it'd always be a party, because I'd imagined the same thing, before realizing that that was a whole other fantasy beyond just living in the house. "I think it might get lonely," I said. "All those shelves and bookcases. Heck, most of the rooms. They'd all be empty if I lived here."

"You'd have to just start filling them up," Gerald said. "Plasma screen. Pool table. A couple mirrors or some shit. I don't know, you'd get a decorator."

He was living in a fantasy for sure, one where we never had to ask Dale for a draw on our paychecks, and where we never got behind on the satellite TV bill. Kirsten was my decorator. "Right now," I said, "I feel like I want to be pouring everything out."

We started hauling wood to the car. I opened the hatchback, and we stuck the two-by-fours and trim pieces down the center, angling them so I'd be able to use the stick shift. The bead board, even when we bent it a little, was still too wide to fit in the car and had to go on the roof. The boards sagged in the middle when we hoisted them up. I only had one bungee cord with me, and we'd already used it to tie down the tailgate. We couldn't find any rope, only some hot pink mason line. Even an extension cord probably would've worked all right.

"One of us has to ride on top," I said. I think Gerald knew that I meant him.

"Rochambeau."

I pointed out that I was the only one with a license.

"You're heavier," he said.

♨

I USED TO think about it more. All those days spent in bed, immobile, stoned on Vicodin, wondering what would've happened had I gone rock instead of paper. But I've come to see that it's silly to worry about stuff like that, the what-ifs, so I've tried to eliminate that kind of thinking, just as I've tried to eliminate other things from my life. I can't say if I'm happier now, but I no longer feel broken, and my head has finally stopped ringing, and for that I'm grateful. My bones only ache when a storm front rolls through.

"Start slow," I yelled to Gerald. "Go gradual."

My face was flat against the wood, my arms stretched wide. My legs dangled off the back of the roof. What I remember is how good it felt to be so foolish. And how so very little, besides that moment, seemed to matter. It was a kind of peace that I hadn't felt in years. I didn't know what was going to happen, only that I'd try and hold on.

Gerald merged off the gravel shoulder and onto the blacktop. He lifted a can of beer out the window and wiggled it around some, which I guess was his way of asking if I wanted any.

"I'm good," I shouted. Gerald said something, but I couldn't hear what it was. Slowly, the can sunk from view. "Turn the radio down," I yelled. "Unless it's something good. Then crank it."

Gerald thought he was driving around forty. That's when I pounded on the roof. I'd told him to keep inching up in speed until I banged on the top of the car, and that'd be as fast as I wanted to go. A few times, he said in his statements, he'd sped up to see if I'd pound on the roof again, so maybe it was closer to fifty.

We were passing through the Nicolet, not far from the fish hatchery, where the trees had been cut back from the road. Even in the hard darkness you could sense those red pines towering along the embankment. The air ripped through my hair and under my t-shirt. I felt like I was flying. I wanted the wind to scour me. Once in a while we'd move through a cloud of bugs and I'd put my face down and listen to them splatting the windshield. Otherwise, I watched the road. I was entranced by the motion, had been fixating on that ever-changing spot where the headlights ended and the darkness began. Gerald stuck his hand out the window and raised his middle finger and let out a howl. The volume on the radio went up. I could feel him pounding on the ceiling of the car. He was absolutely right. We had a moment there where the night seemed to be humming, and we felt like outlaws, like invincible men.

Then came the quick flash of the deer, and the thud of it hitting the side of the car.

WHEN GERALD SWERVED—one way, then overcorrecting—the boards shifted, and a terrible whip-snap pitched me from the roof. If I think back to it now, though he must have only been a blur, I remember seeing Gerald as I fell. He was leaning forward, with his chest against the steering wheel, and his eyes fixed on the rearview. I wanted to yell to him, scream that he was looking the wrong way, that I was over here, but I couldn't. I remember feeling like I was gasping for breath, like someone was dunking me under the water. I wanted Gerald to turn and look me in the eyes, flash that same smile he must've had just a second before, during all our glory. I thought that if he saw me some sort of safety line would come taut and catch me. But I could feel things shrinking away. Gerald was staring into the mirror, at the cartwheeling deer. "Lit up red," he later said. "From the brake lights."

❧

KIRSTEN WAS IN the hospital room when I woke up. She was sitting in a vinyl armchair by the window and reading a magazine. She had her hair in pigtails, which were my favorite, and she was wearing khaki pants, part of her uniform from the Evergreen.

I sensed being in the road, smelling the asphalt and wondering if Darren had paved that section of highway. I remembered the sound of feet slapping the ground as the paramedics ran toward me. The doctors told me I was out cold the whole time, but I remember Gerald being there and talking to me and saying that I'd make it.

"Hey," Kirsten said, when she noticed me staring. "Look who's awake." She got up from the chair and came over and held my hand. She rubbed my fingers and smiled at me, searching my face, which felt swollen as a balloon.

"Am I okay?" I asked.

Kirsten shook her head yes and started to cry. "Sorry," she said, when I asked her to stop. She wiped her eyes and smiled for me and tried to seem cheerful. "You will be," she said. "You're alive."

The first step in building our house, after subcontracting the excavation work, was putting together the forms for the foundation. Gerald helped. It was tedious and hard labor, but we moved our way through it—knocking in stakes, leveling the boards, cutting and bending and tying the rebar together.

We were measuring one of the corners, making sure we'd kept the forms square. "I've got forty and three-eighths," I said, letting the tape retract. "We're close."

"I can live with close," Gerald said. "Close is fine."

I smiled when I heard that. Math that was approximate. For a while I even took what Gerald said as some truism for life. I thought of that day while in the hospital. We had gotten so that we couldn't even touch each other. Kirsten started playing with my hair. She tested my forehead with the back of her hand. My collarbone was broken, my leg stabilized by titanium pins. I wanted to reach up and take her hand and put it against my cheek.

"I'm glad you woke up before I had to go," she said.

"Me too." I was numb on painkillers, so for a moment it seemed maybe it had been worth it, just to be like that with her again.

After the ambulance took me away that night, Gerald got arrested. He spent twenty hours in jail, only a few blocks from the hospital. Dale fired us both, though he hired Gerald back on short-term to help him finish the lake house. I went out and looked at it once, probably a year or so after it was completed. The owners had it up for sale already. All the blinds were drawn, and on the deck the furniture was stacked and covered with a blue tarp. Down by the water, an aluminum rowboat sat upside down, the hull blanketed in pine needles.

Kirsten went to the chair and grabbed her purse, and she promised to come back in the morning.

"Don't promise," I said. I didn't want her to do that.

She found an apartment in Kemper and was out of the house before I'd even been released from the hospital. Gerald called me a few times after I went home, and couldn't stop apologizing, couldn't stop saying he'd make it for a visit sometime, even though he'd have to hitchhike. When it was time for physical therapy, my mom and dad put me in the back of their minivan and drove me to town. Sometimes we'd stop on the way back and get some carry-out and go to my empty house, where my mom would set the table, and my dad would plate all the food, and we'd sit and eat in silence, or maybe talk about the weather, or how good the fried chicken was. Kirsten and I had accepted an offer on the place and were waiting for the closing date. My half was already spent, the price of my trauma.

Once, at therapy, I thought I saw Darren. He had on a camouflage shirt and was sitting at one of the padded benches. He was pulling a sock over his nub leg, prepping it for his prosthetic. When he looked up, I saw I was wrong, that he was just a stranger. I didn't know whether he'd served or not, but I gave him a little salute.

The day I went and looked at the lake house, I also drove past Gerald's place. We'd been up late the night before and had already said some beer-soaked good-byes. My little car was packed tight with whatever I had left. I'd planned on stopping one last time, but as I got near I decided to just keep going.

The Howitzer sat at the end of Gerald's driveway. He'd painted the whole sculpture primer gray, which took away from all that wood, though it still looked good, it still stood out. The telescope was mounted just where he'd shown me it'd go.

Instead of getting a cloth flag, Gerald had painted an American flag on a square of the bead board, and he'd hung it from the Howitzer's barrel. He'd made a sign that read BRING THE TROOPS HOME, a yellow ribbon sticker in each of the corners. To what, I wondered, speeding by. Bring them home to what? In real life, the Howitzer had a range of almost twenty miles. I put my foot on the gas, knowing I'd have to go at least that far to be safe.

The Golden Torch

MY FATHER WANTED new shoes, a pair with Velcro instead of laces. Shoes were something you had to drive into town for, and my father no longer drove, unless it was just to the end of the driveway to get the mail. Before I came over, he'd made me a pot of coffee, though he wasn't supposed to drink it anymore. While he finished up his breakfast dishes, I sipped down half a cup and then set the mug next to the sink so that he could have what was left. He took a big gulp and dipped the mug into the sudsy water, squeaked the washcloth around a few times and then rinsed. I grabbed the towel off his shoulder and dried.

"What else?" I asked.

"My billfold is on my dresser," he said, pulling the plug from the drain, shuddering the pipes.

Next to my father's wallet sat a piece of paper, a to-do list. My father's bedroom, just like the rest of the house, was also once my mother's. This was in the long-ago life before my brother Ken electrocuted himself on a jobsite by swinging his aluminum ladder into a distribution line, back in a time when my mother still squeezed my father's ass when she wanted to fluster him in public, and back before I ever knew Barbara, or how after so much matrimonial right, there could be so much wrong.

Now my mom lived with her sister in Boca Raton and sent cards on my birthday, always with a little cash taped inside, and sometimes pictures of her and her incredibly ember-like tan. Barbara, my ex-wife, owned a lake house the next county over, and we rarely talked, unless it was something about Kelly, our daughter. Our conversations usually ended with, "I just thought you might want to know." They could have easily begun the same way. Last either one of us had heard, Kelly was driving a car more expensive than anything we'd ever owned and dancing under the name Diamond.

My father had written some simple, straightforward tasks at the beginning of his to-do list—*TRASH OUT* the first, *GET SHOES* the second— and he'd made sure to underline what time he needed to be at the fire drill that night—*7 PM*—but as the list went on, it became less business-like and more a counting of resolutions, like something you'd write on New Year's. My father kept his room as clean as a showcase at a department store. I'd rifled through it a million times when I was a kid, as had Ken—revved by the chance of finding Christmas presents in the closet, or the skin flicks that sometimes showed up under the bed, or later, in high school, the cigarettes and money we lifted from Mom's nightstand.

Now my father wanted to turn off the TV more. He wanted to eat slower, set an exercise routine, be thankful. *ENJOY THE NOW*, he'd written. *NO MORE LISTS*.

In the car, still in the driveway, I asked him, leaving the question wide open, "How you coming along?"

My father was particular. He was the kind of man who drew outlines of his tools on the pegboard in the garage, and the kind who swept up after each project. He believed, though he'd left much chaos in the wake of himself, that the world could be kept orderly and neat. He'd driven a grader for the county roads crew all his life, and when the guys wrote on his retirement plaque—*Verlan, he could level a dime*—they got it pretty close, because my father had the pigheadedness and patience to go at something until he got it exactly how he wanted. If he said he wanted a pair of Velcro shoes, we were not looking for any pair, but a pair that he'd already envisioned, right down to the pattern on the tread.

"I'm making it," my father said with a groan, buckling his seat-belt. "High humidity tonight." As head of the Wolf River Rural Fire Department, my father was going to lead us that night, me and seven other volunteers, as we burned Carol's Golden Torch and practiced putting out the large-scale blaze with the pump trucks. "Should be pretty safe," he said.

My father and I were certified to teach CPR and every winter we'd offer a class at the town hall, just down the road from Carol's bar. There'd been a lot of wasted evenings at the Golden Torch—slump-shouldered and vulgar nights, many of which my dad and I, though at different phases in history, had taken part in. But Carol's had been out of business for years now, and the bank wanted the land cleared. Wolf River already had six other taverns barely on their feet.

Not many of us on the team had had much training beyond the basics, and mostly we just dealt with the occasional burn barrel fire gone bad. Sometimes, so far from all else, we were first responders to the dire—an old local bent over a weighted snow shovel and clutching his chest, or a bad accident at one of the notorious intersections.

"We'll set you out on the second hose with Digger," my father said. "Run the line around the back of Teddy's."

Teddy's meant the Stargazer, the bar next door, which the town board wanted protected. It had been a trading post way back in the fur days, and now it was part bar, part convenience store.

"I'll use the curtain nozzle," I said.

Teddy and Carol had run the Stargazer together until they'd divorced, which is when Teddy gave Carol the Golden Torch—a smaller, ranch-style place just across the parking lot. "I'll let it rain," I said. "As much as the pump can give me."

I drove the back way, up and then over. It was the same, mileage-wise, but it took longer and wound through the moraines and jig-jagged through a maze of ninety-degree turns across the farmlands. My father watched the ditch streak past. Over the past year, I'd noticed something in my father—a vacating of sorts. When I visited I sometimes found him just sitting at the kitchen table, his hands folded in his lap, waiting for something to happen.

"I saw your list," I said.

My father had been making lists his whole life—parts he needed for a carpentry project, or what groceries to stock up on during the next run to town, debts he owed and things he was ahead on. But this one seemed different. I knew, because I did it too, especially when I wanted to make a change. QUIT THIS, QUIT THAT. RAKE THE LEAVES. WASH THE CAR. For my father it was one more attempt at a kind of order in his life, an order, which I knew, was impossible for a Hollenberg.

"Always something to do," my father said.

"Never ends," I said, trying to sound in total agreement. "Not much crossed off, though."

"Give me a chance," my father said. He turned my way, leaning back against the door, his eyebrows—white and long and uneven—raised like some drawbridge waiting for the next wiseass to sail beneath. For a second, it was as if we'd returned to our normalcy, where every back and forth between us was too true and not funny enough. "I just wrote it last night," he said. "Got the trash out before I even went to bed."

As we got close to town, the brown of the springtime fields, bit-by-bit, turned to the green of nitrogen-rich lawns. The houses were mostly modest and practical, though sometimes the lawns sprawled for acres. Soon I was slowing. In thirty miles my father and I had passed only two cars, but at the intersection just ahead of us the traffic cut back and forth so heavy I thought we'd never have a chance of joining.

We sat silently at the stop sign, my father looking north while I looked south, toward town. A space began opening my way, and when I turned to see if I had a chance the other direction—when I saw that I did not—I simply watched my father as he waited to give me an all clear. I stared at him, eased by the fact that he wasn't staring back, and I began to think about fire. A flashover, which signaled the start of a structure fire, sucked the air from a room. There was, with flame, a point of no return. And like all those trees browned by the emerald ash borer, I was sure I had been turned to tinder.

Part of my dad's jacket was puffed out and bunched up under his seatbelt, and it made him appear smaller than he was. I reached over and pulled it straight.

"After this one," he said, "looks like an opening."

"Still good?" I asked after the car whizzed past, though I could already see as much.

"Still good," he said.

⁂

BEFORE TRYING THE Payless at the mini-mall, my father had us stop at Joseph's, a family-run store Mom had taken Ken and me to at the start of every school year. My father believed in downtown, a short two blocks that hadn't been much for even longer than Carol's had been empty. I don't remember many of the other businesses that used to fill Main Street. Except for Joseph's, and the bank on the corner, and Rudzinski's Hardware, all the other buildings that weren't empty were now home to antique stores, cheap-as-shit and dust-filled places that people passing through from Milwaukee and Chicago couldn't resist.

"Here, Dad," I said, taking the front door from him as he tried holding it open for me.

"Go," he said. He had one arthritic hand still on the door, and his other was waving me ahead.

We both stood there, waiting for the other, each with our gentlemanly points to prove. "I got it," I finally said, gently pushing him forward, though I could tell by his expression that I should have just taken his offer.

Joseph's was the kind of store that had serious woodwork, dark trim along the floor and ornate molding up at the ceiling, something my father appreciated. A pair of worn, leather chairs—deep and sturdy pieces that would clean up nice and last forever—faced each other in the center of the room. The men's shoes filled one wall, ladies' another. We were welcomed to the store by a young man, some college-age kid wearing an ironed shirt and tie, an outfit that seemed silly and aggressive for where we were shopping. The kid had been holding a pair of sleek basketball shoes, turning them over in his hands, when my father and I walked into the store, but now he was standing at attention in front of us, his hands clasped behind himself, wondering what he could do us for.

"I'm hunting for some shoes without laces," my father said. "Something with Velcro tabs. No knots to tie."

"Like maybe a slip-on," the sales kid said, glancing at the men's shoes, then back at my father.

My father made a noise, one that said sort of yes, but mostly no. I felt a similar noise roil inside myself, though mine was mostly *oh, no*. My father held his hands up in front of himself, trying to give us a picture of what he was looking for. "Not quite," he said. "More sturdy. A shoe I can go off-road with, something I can put some mileage on."

My father had always loved to walk along the river. He loved to fish. He'd made a trail from the back edge of the yard and down through the woods, where at the shoreline it joined another trail, an ancient one, one that the Menominee had taken all the way up to Lake Superior. It had always been easy for my father to slip out of the house, and many times when I was younger, and my mother thought it time for him to come home, I was the one sent to bring my father back. My father had a few favorite spots that he often went to, though sometimes I never found him, even after I'd marched all the way past the train trestle. Other times he'd be close, as close to the house as possible while still being alongside the river, just sitting on a log, his pants rolled up, his socks off, soaking his feet.

I'd sit next to him and tug at his arm, saying *Mom, Mom, Mom*, knowing now how annoying I must have sounded, knowing now that what I saw in his eyes then was not him just being tired, like he'd said, but something much more complex and storm-like.

"Okay," the sales kid said. "I think I'm feeling you." He was aiming his index fingers at us. "I got a Rockport to try. There's a couple New Balance you might like."

"Sure," my father said. "With Velcro."

"Not a lot," the kid said. "But let me show you."

"And white, right?" I asked. "Didn't you say white?"

"I don't want black," my father said. "Black shoes are for dressing up. For big occasions." He pointed at the kid. "You should know that."

Looking down, I noticed the kid was wearing a pair of black dress shoes.

❧

MY FATHER LIKED to discipline Ken and me at the river. He'd march us out the back door, usually with the warning that he had some serious words for us. Sometimes he pulled us along by an earlobe. When Ken and I got caught stealing candy bars from the grocery, or even stupider things like smashing canisters of spray paint with a sledgehammer, splattering Caution Yellow over the lawn furniture and our faces, our father pushed us ahead—not so much with his hands, but his pace—so that we'd have to run a little while he listed the myriad ways in which we were totally and completely shits.

After Mom caught Ken and me smoking behind the garage, my father had us move about a million wheelbarrows of old river stone he'd dug up over the years in his garden. We just moved it from one side of the yard to the other, one pile to the next. When I was sixteen, only a few days after I got my license, when I'd crumpled the family car in a ditch, my father hiked me up to Twenty Day Rapid while openly contemplating a future he saw coming, one where I'd pissed everything away and still hadn't learned my lessons.

My father and I had stopped at the bottom of the rapid, and we were watching the long, boulder-strewn cascade as it pooled up in front of us. Below, the river curved slowly to the east, where we'd just come from, and its tannin water was dotted with foam. The sun had started to get low on the horizon, casting everything along the shore—the reeds and nettles and us—in a warm, fiery light.

"What do you see?" my father asked me then.

"Stone fly," I said. "Midge. Not sure."

I couldn't tell what it was that had hatched, but the fish were rising all over the place. Above our own heads, clouds of mosquitoes hovered, buzzing like an electrical line.

"Well," he said. "We got some choices, right?" He'd been talking choices the entire walk, had been proclaiming that they were all we had, and that mine had been lousy. "So choose," he said, holding the tackle box out to me.

I'd begun to move up the trail, bored already, done already, staring at the ground as if it would somehow flare to life like a television set turned on. I'd shoved in the station wagon's whole right panel, made it undrivable, and not a scratch was on me. My only excuse was that I wasn't paying attention, but I was annoyed that I even needed an excuse at all. I stood at the river, my back to my father, and I wasn't listening, though he was talking directly to me.

"Jesus!" I said, interrupting whatever he was saying. "Just give me one. Give me whatever one it is."

I was waiting for something, like maybe a huff and the sound of the fly case opening, a signal that my father had given up on that day's lecture. But then I flinched, my body knowing before I did. My father's fiberglass pole whistled through the air, slapping me across my sunburned neck.

I knelt on the dirt, with a hand on my sticky and welted skin, just staring at him. He stared back at me, his rod angled out to the side, hanging there as if he was letting out line with the current, watching me drift downstream. When I ran for home, he reached for my arm as I passed him, catching me long enough to say my name before I pulled free.

❧

THE SHOE KID had gone to the back room to retrieve my father's size in the one Velcro shoe Joseph's had. As he waited, my father wandered along the rest of the men's casuals, standing close, leaning in like he was looking into a car's glare-filled window at a car lot. Never once did he pick up another shoe, never once looked at their soles. When he stopped next to a full-length mirror, one that my own reflection filled from half a store away, our faces were framed side by side. I watched my father's eyes scanning each stitch, looking for something, and I could tell then that I didn't, like my father had many times said, have any blessed clue.

"No half-sizes," the sales kid said, rejoining us. "I brought an eight and a nine."

Before my father even had a chance to sit down, the sales kid had unwrapped a shoe, un-Velcroed it, and thumbed it open for him. "This is the eight," he said. He took the shoe by the toe and spun it so my father could slip right in.

"No eight and a half?" my father asked, heeling off his old shoe, which was hardly worn.

The kid was sitting on one of those stools that places like Payless didn't have anymore, or never did, the kind angled in front so he could help my father pull the laces tight. My father wore thin black dress socks, the kind I would've put a million holes in already. Once my father's shoe was snugged up, the kid squeezed along the length of my father's foot, checking the fit. He patted the back of my father's calf and slid back. "Take a stroll," he said.

My father made a loop around the room and over to the mirror I had been watching him in, and he stood up on his toes. "No eight-and-a-half?" he asked again.

"Not right now," the kid answered. "Well," he continued, perhaps assuming it could be that easy, "what's the verdict?"

"They look nice," I said, hoping it would make up for something.
My father went back to expressing himself in noises.

✨

"Should we stop quick?" I asked as we passed the mini-mall. "We can always take those back." He'd gone with the nines, the larger size, though his body had clearly reached its shrinking phase.

My father sat with the shoebox on his lap, with his old shoes inside, looking much like he did whenever I came by and found him at the kitchen table.

"They probably won't have anything," he said, which somehow seemed to me to mean yes, please stop, though I kept driving. "I don't think they make what I'm looking for," he said, which I learned wasn't true the next trip to town, when I stopped and checked.

"Wouldn't hurt to look," I said.

"Neither would lunch."

At B.B. Jack's, an old supper club that had pretty decent sand-wiches, my father and I seated ourselves in a dim, quiet dining room that filled to overflowing during Friday night fish fries. We were two of four customers, the others a pair of potato farmers with dark, silt-dusted skin, finishing a couple of hamburgers up at the bar. Half the lights in the restaurant hadn't been turned on, and my father and I were near the meridian of light and dark. When the waitress brought us menus and noted the lighting, she apologized, which we insisted was unnecessary.

"Something to drink?" the waitress asked.

My father and I both ordered Diet Cokes. "And a coffee," I added, when I heard my father wilting. "Cream," I said. "No sugar."

I took off my jacket and hung it on the back of my chair. My father unwrapped the paper napkin from his silverware and smoothed it flat against the table. He rocked onto one butt cheek so he could fish out the checkbook from his back pocket. He slid a pen from the checkbook and uncapped it, then scribbled a blue oblong on the napkin.

"What you working on?" I asked. He was chewing on his lip.

"Thinking about tonight," my father said. "I just want to make sure we take our time. Know what everyone is doing. Check off everything as we go along."

My father began writing the names of the people on the team, beginning with his own. He'd already reworked this list a half-dozen times, I'm sure. When he got to the bottom of the roster, he started working back up it, putting a colon behind each name, bottom dot first. After that he watched me take a sip of coffee.

"Okay," I said, knowing he wanted to talk it through with me. "Start at the top."

"I only know what I'm doing when I know what the rest of you are doing."

"Okay then," I said. "What's everybody doing?"

My father started filling in tasks. Digger and I would be together. Charlie Preboski and Lester Dicky had the attack line. Once it was pumping, the intake station just needed someone to sit close and watch the drafting hose.

"I was thinking I'd put Melnick's kid on that," my father said. "Keep him out of the way."

It all sounded fine, and I knew that no matter how much my father tried to choreograph it all, he was dealing with secondhand equipment and a bunch of guys who were eager to let the flames get high, guys who'd have beer-filled coolers sitting in the beds of their pickup trucks at the town hall, and it was all likely to get scary at some point.

"We'll keep an eye on each other," I assured him.

"This is real," my father told me.

Our waitress had shouldered our food, and she was rounding the corner at the bar. My father was right. Digger had spent the past two days yanking shingles and tearing out extra wood from Carol's so there'd be less fuel. Farther along in the fire drill, we'd punch open a hole in the roof to direct and pull the fire upwards—a procedure that would corral the flames, while at the same time stoking them. I sat up. "How come no more lists?" I finally asked.

My father waited until our plates were in front of us and I'd cut halfway through my chicken breast. "It's not no more lists like this one," he said. While my father had given up some things, like coffee, mostly, and his late-night bowl of ice cream, he still hadn't parted from salt, and he showered it across his hissing French fries. He, expert of choices, was also good with justifications. "This isn't a list," he said. "This is organization."

A few summers back the fire department got a call for a car-meets-tree just north of the reservation. I was mowing a field out on County M, so it was quicker for me to drive straight to the scene, and I beat everyone but Charlie Preboski there. A few others had already stopped and were directing traffic, the rest wandering in the road, shaking their heads and covering their faces. The forest is unlogged on that stretch of highway, and the trees come right up to the roadside. The car lay on its side, and I could only see the warped undercarriage as I approached. On the other side of the car, I found Charlie scrambling around on his knees, trying to save a life. Three teenagers, all girls: one thrown from the car, the only one who survived, the other two crushed inside. I could hear the rescue van and fire trucks wailing toward us.

"She lives on my street," Charlie said, one hand holding her head, the other firm on her chest, trying to stanch the blood.

This could be Kelly, I thought. Later the car had to be cut from the tree. I tried calling my daughter that night, but the number I had no longer worked, and I didn't want to call Barbara for the new one.

My father's organization was crucial on that scene. These were girls of our community—they were neighbors, babysitters, honor students—and Charlie was not the only person in the department to know one or all of them. Without my father's direction, we would have operated full-pedal on emotion, rather than triage and protocol. We likely would have lost everyone, trying to save all of them.

"Instead of lists," my father said, "I should have written down No more answers." He'd folded his hands, and he took a second for a private, silent grace before his meal. "There's no missing piece," he said. "Don't have it, don't want it. That's how it should be."

Back at my place, I had a cat, a television, and a radio—things to make noise or be near when I needed that. I had a pile of coupons weighted down with a river rock on the kitchen counter, most of which had expired. To come across them in the paper and simply pass them by seemed wasteful and lazy, as stupid as passing up an easy dollar, and I heard my father's voice, heard my own and a million others saying as much, so I cut them out every week. But somehow I was no good at taking it to the next step, and I hardly used a coupon or shopped for the deal, and sometimes I let bills pass due as I stared at their unopened envelopes for days on end. There are probably some sitting next to the coupons now. They are right next to my refrigerator, which has a couple of pictures stuck to it: one of Kelly, the summer she turned ten, sticking out her Kool-Aid blue tongue, and one of me, right there at my own personal apex, trying to do three things at once—keep my mirrored sunglasses from sliding off into the river, balance a can of beer, and hold up the biggest brown trout I'd ever landed—my pregnant wife behind the camera.

My father took a fry and scraped the excess tartar sauce from the edges of his sandwich. "So this is the new me," he said, through a mouthful of food. "Eat well, exercise. Enjoy what I have."

"Be happy," I said.

"A good, simple life."

❦

WE HAD TESTED all the radio channels. Digger and I were ready with our line, hoses charged, valves dripping. We were dressed in full turn-out gear, my own steel-toed rubber boots already an inch deep in puddle. My father and Jim Larson, Wolf River pitching all-star and one time minor league promise, stood at the front doorway of Carol's, the actual door having been scrapped earlier by Digger. A red light, rotating atop the pumper truck, threw shadows rhythmically against the tavern's façade, casting my father and Jim out of proportion.

Charlie and Lester were already inside, stacking a little pile of kindling at the base of the back wall. My father had picked Jim to set the flares, largely because Jim was no longer the asshole he used to be, which now made him a pretty dependable and straightforward guy. He also hit three home runs in last season's softball championship, winning us a two-tiered trophy to put in our fire hall.

My father and Jim peeled away from each other—my father toward the rescue van, and Jim into Carol's. As chief, my father wore a white fire hat, a contrast to our yellow, and I traced it as he crossed the gravel parking lot and then took post at command. A moment later, Jim stepped back into view at the doorway and flashed us a half-wave—the fire was alive. Charlie, Lester and Jim stepped outside and waited with the rest of us.

"Ten-twelve," my father said over the radio, code for "stand by."

At the river the swallows were flitting from out below the bridge and looping into the dying night. A few had tucked their homes under the eaves at Teddy's, just above my station. Teddy stood in his parking lot, an apron tied at his waist, his arms splayed across the shoulders of his new wife and their youngest son. Our crowd would grow all night. Already, just as the interior of the tavern was beginning to glow, half a dozen cars were spaced out along the shoulder of the road. Some people, including Carol, had even brought lawn chairs.

My father called the first team inside. One after another, wearing Kevlar hoods and SCBA masks and packs, Ed Wulagert, Ron Reynebeau, and Chip Van Boxtel got down on their knees and began crawling into the Golden Torch, pulling their hose along, smoke venting thick and black above them. I'd seen other men of the community crawl across that threshold before, only they were usually leaving for home, headed toward their own catastrophes.

I'd gotten to practice with the attack team during our last training burn, two years back when the Melnicks wanted to get rid of their outbuilding, so I knew the otherworldly experience of sitting in a room on fire. My body had said save yourself, just like I guessed Ed, Ron, and Chip's were saying right then. Flee. But my mind said follow the protocols, remember what we'd simulated, use the acronyms. All else seemed to fade away then, and I worried only about me, the men on my line, and the fire—a strange, heated reprieve from the outside world, a reprieve I longed to find again.

Inside Carol's, the flames had climbed to the ceiling and had starting trailing across it. Unable to take a regular peaked shape, the fire layered itself along the ceiling, so that the flames looked like a shifting, orange cloud. Above Carol's, despite the darkening sky, heat waves warped the air. The burning wood snapped and crackled. Already the fire had started bucking up, and if the guys didn't watch it, the room would superheat.

"Let's open that stream a little more," my father called out. "Second team, go ahead."

Digger and I began dampening the outside of Carol's, hitting the same wall the fire consumed on the inside. It was a good, conservative call, especially with a team inside. Everyone trusted my father, and so did I, as much as I could—not completely, but substantially more than he trusted me.

My father let Digger and me run for a bit, and then eased us back. Once the guys inside regained some control, they were on their own again. My father wanted them to get as much practice in as they could. On a normal call, we'd try to save the building as quickly as possible, but at Carol's there was nothing to be saved. In fact, on this night, our goal was the opposite—we wanted a complete loss.

After Ed and Ron and Chip put out the initial fire, after my father had us re-light and re-extinguish it again, after a group of us had a chance to climb a ladder to the roof—which is something I can't do without thinking about my brother—and cut a hole through the plywood with our Eckert hooks and pick axes, and after it was well past dark, we lit the fire one grand last time. Then we let it go.

When the flames began pouring out from Carol's windows, my father pulled everyone away from their posts and had the entire department stand in front of the bar for a photo, which Teddy snapped for us. I knelt in the front row, while my father stood behind me in the second. Above us the sky glowed yellow and orange, a nice little halo over our moment. Some of the people on the side of the road clapped and cheered for us, and it felt pretty good, even if I thought it was somewhat undeserved.

My father reached down and squeezed my shoulders, which I scrunched up instictively, wanting him off me. As the rest of the department started returning to the fire, my father held on, and I finally dropped my shoulders, letting him rub them a little. I was sweaty and sore, and I'd been awake, like him, since dawn. His hands were damp and cool, and he used his big, scarred thumbs to push deep. I moaned, wordlessly and cow-like.

I spent the rest of the night with Digger keeping watch on Teddy's, thinking a million thoughts under those towering and hypnotic flames. When all was finally ruin and charcoal, my father made the call to pack it in. We opened all the lines wide, a full deluge, pushing the pump engine hard.

WHILE MY FATHER and a few others stayed behind to watch for hot-spots, some of the rest of us went down to the river and passed Chip's flask around. There were a few rocks to sit on and there was a homemade river gauge—a two-by-four painted in five-inch color blocks—jammed into the shoreline. Chip shined his pocket flashlight along the river's edge. The river level measured blue, maybe three feet deep, or just a little more, which wasn't promising, especially so soon in the year. By the end of the summer, the Wolf would likely be but a trickle, hard to fish, unless you knew the feeder springs. And even then.

When he was ready to go, my father walked down to the landing to get me.

"There he is," Charlie said, feeling pretty lively. Chip joined in, clinking the side of his bottle with his flashlight. I whistled softly at my dad, as if I was calling for his encore.

"Looking for a ride?" I asked, as he gave me a hand off my rock.

"Wouldn't mind," he said.

"I think I'll hit it myself," Charlie said. He offered to take my father home for me, but I said it was fine.

I started leading our little group up the riverbank. "Heck of a night," I said.

When the Melnick kid had flushed the pumper truck, the water had run off down the path, washing out a few spots, and I was wishing I had Chip's light. I was just about to ask him to shine it my way when I heard my father slip and fall.

My father had splashed into the pitch-black water and was dog-paddling, kicking hard. Chip flashed his light on the river, and I yelled for my father to stand up, even though I knew it could be a bad thing to do if the current was too strong. My father was puffing air, as if he was giving birth. His arms churned the water, like a boat motor trimmed too high. His movements began slowing, and then he simply turned onto his back and drifted downstream.

I had jumped in and was almost to him.

"My shoes!" my father cried. He had balled himself up trying to keep his shoes on, and he looked like a fishing bobber with something biting at the hook.

I grabbed my father's collar and swung him into an eddy. One of his shoes popped to the surface nearby, the other one still half on his foot. My father had swallowed some water, and he coughed and tried to catch his breath. I reached out and bumped the half-submerged shoe into the eddy with us. The cold water seeped through my clothes, enough so that I started panting from the shock of it. I wanted to plunge under, where it was dark and icy and quiet, but I had one arm wrapped around my father, and I could feel his heart pounding hard.

The river was shallow enough to touch bottom, but instead my father and I just floated there, with Chip's flashlight in our eyes.

"I got you," I said, holding tight. "We're not going anywhere."

A Chat with Eliot

TYLER MCMANN INTERVIEWS ELIOT TREICHEL.

TYLER: I'm Tyler McMann and I'm interviewing Eliot Treichel today about his forthcoming story collection, *Close is Fine*, from Ooligan Press. It's coming out in the fall, is that right?

ELIOT: Yeah, I think November 1st.

TYLER: Great. A little bit of a back story: I think I originally read "Good Potato Soil," a story from this collection, not quite ten years ago but probably more than six years or so, when I was editing a small journal in Idaho—so I'm kind of curious to hear the history of the project. Where did it start, how long has it been going on for and so forth?

ELIOT: How long it's been going is debatable I guess. ["Good Potato Soil"] is the oldest story. I think I started the first draft in 1998; I had this idea, as I had just finished college and wanted to be a writer, and [felt I] needed to write a collection [of stories]. The first draft [of "Good Potato Soil"] is pretty different from what you see today; there were aliens in it and all sorts of things…

TYLER: [Laughter].

ELIOT: So if you start at 1998, that would be about fifteen years it took to get the book done. The driving force over all those years was really that I wanted to write about this place where I grew up, after having left. [And I was] trying to talk about this rural place in the middle of nowhere, but that everyone who lived there often referred to as the center of the universe; and I was trying to articulate that [aspect of it]. At one point I referred to it as my love song to Wisconsin. ["Good Potato Soil"] got rejected at so many places, even after I got lots of feedback; I think it was first published about seven years [after I wrote it].

TYLER: Yeah, I've been here for four years, and was away for a year, so I think it would have to be in the neighborhood of six or seven years [when I first saw it in Idaho]. I was there when it came out, I was working at that journal, and I think it was one of the first stories I read while I was there. I never forgot it, though; it was one of the best stories we ever published!

ELIOT: That's great!

TYLER: There was a line in ["Good Potato Soil"], and I think it made into to the [forthcoming] book, about "silence becoming its own sort of unbearable noise," and I've never forgotten that sentence throughout the years. I've thought of it many times and kind of cribbed it in things that I've written. [Laughter]. It's one of those phrases that just stick with you.

ELIOT: Yeah! Good.

TYLER: I've stuck my foot in my mouth a few times getting frustrated and saying collections of stories are sort of a hodge-podge of everything one person has written, and that there should be more [to it] when binding them into a book. Now, [in *Close is Fine*] the stories are united by setting, but [there isn't] a real narrative that leads you from one story to the next; yet it's clear to readers of the book that there is a unity to the collection. How do you see the connection between the stories?

ELIOT: I tried to connect them in two ways. One, there's the tavern, the "Stargazer," that appears in several stories, and in some stories it's front and center while in other stories it's just sort of off to the periphery. I think that's one of the things that unites the stories.

TYLER: Right.

ELIOT: The second one is the river, or the rivers. I think every story has a river in it somewhere. And I think when I first started, I wanted it to be all these different spots along the river, and the river would be like the thread that connected it together; the spots sort of changed, but I think there's the place, [or setting], like you said, that connects it all together. It is set in northern Wisconsin and there are some real town names in the collection, but I definitely moved them around and renamed them, so it's not like if you looked on a map it would all match up.

TYLER: [Laughter] I can't necessarily go to the Stargazer and get a beer if I'm in the neighborhood.

ELIOT: No, you can't go to that bar with that exact title, but without saying exactly where, there is a place where two highways cross, with dollar bills that people have written things on up on the wall, and where people have laughed, with a convenience store next to it. And it is the oldest building in that area; it was originally a general store back in the day, now it's a bar, part gas station, that sort of thing. So if you know where to go, you can find places that match up.

TYLER: Right on. I'll have to get those from you afterward! On that note, I'm really curious about your influences, and what's really interesting to me about your collection is that this focus on a rural American setting has a history of [being used] in a sort of Flannery O'Connor gothic vein, and also more bucolic kinds of literature. But yours has a grittier, sort of hard-drinking and working-class aspect that reminds me of a Raymond Carver, social-realist vein. So I was curious what you were thinking about when you wrote these stories and put them together.

ELIOT: Raymond Carver was definitely one of the first writers I started reading. When I first was in college, I needed a class, and had a friend who suggested [a fiction-writing class], and I thought it sounded cool and kind of fun and easy, and [in the class] I wrote a story, and felt like "Wow, this makes sense to me." The writers we focused on who kind of hooked me were Raymond Carver, Amy Hempel, and even Sherman Alexie, his collection *The Lone Ranger and Tonto Fist Fight in Heaven*, and then *Jesus' Son* had a pretty profound effect on me.

TYLER: That makes sense.

ELIOT: I read all of those when I was much younger, put them away, forgot

about them, and was working on the collection. I started reading more experimental writers and tried to be more stylistic for a
while, and then that fell away. [After] I had been working on the
collection for a while, things that really started to make it congeal
were [first] getting "Good Potato Soil" published, which started
an avalanche, but then I came across Lee K. Abbott, who I had
never read before. I'm not sure how I heard of him, but I started
reading a collection of his new and selected works, and something
about his writing really made sense to me. [It helped me] really
understand what I wanted to do as far as voice goes, grittiness, etc.
So while Raymond Carver is probably an influence, and it would
be interesting to look back, I last read him twenty years ago.

TYLER: Yes. So, I'd like to stick with the setting thing a little bit. Do you
feel like there are other representatives in fiction or in general
literature of the northern Wisconsin/Great Lakes area? I kept
thinking of "The Wreck of the Edmund Fitzgerald." [Laughter].
Or novels or stories that weren't necessarily set there. But did you
have anything in mind, a kind of aesthetic that you identify with
that region?

ELIOT: I bet there are some writers I haven't heard of that know about
that [aesthetic]. I think maybe the closest thing I've read recently
was Knockemstiff. I think the author is Donald Ray Pollock. But,
I wasn't so much influenced by other writers; it was just that place
that I lived in.

TYLER: [Nodding]. Yeah.

ELIOT: There is that Wilco song, and then the documentary, *I Am Trying
to Break Your Heart*, the refrain of which sort of stuck in my head,
and I thought, well, if I could just do that, if I could make it kind
of sad. That's what I wanted to do, and I thought if I could do
that, it would work; and I don't know if I achieved that, or if it
got filtered through [the collection], and it came out differently.

TYLER: Uh-huh. Yeah.

ELIOT: But there isn't a "Wisconsin" book that I know of.

TYLER: And I think that's one of [*Close is Fine*'s] strengths, is that it's
fresh in that way; it's rural American, but not the South or cow-
boys, I really appreciated that about it.

ELIOT: Can I throw in one thing?

TYLER: Yeah!

ELIOT: When I first started on the collection and knew what I wanted to do, *That 70's Show* came out, which is set in Wisconsin, and I was just so mad, because I thought, "that isn't the Wisconsin I know."

TYLER: [Laughter] Yeah.

ELIOT: So like many states, Wisconsin is full of stereotypes, like "they just eat cheese and drink beer and people are overweight." You know, Green Bay Packers. And some of those stereotypes are true to a certain degree, but I wanted to try to articulate the place that I knew, which was different.

TYLER: Cool. Let me talk about craft for a minute; I just want to hear a little bit about your process: where the stories start. It seems to me like you're interested in landscape and place but I wasn't sure if that was the genesis, or if you were thinking more [about] characters, or even language. And [also], what's the turnaround time; are you more linear [in writing], and do you have a shitty-first-draft or a perfectionist kind of model?

ELIOT: I really don't like first drafts! They're tough, that part of the process feels pretty miserable to me. But once I have something [I like] I can go back and revise, and I actually really like revising. I usually start a draft, go all the way through, until I get to an ending point, and then put it away. Then I come back and work on it. ["Good Potato Soil"] took a long time to get right. But some of the later stories I wrote took two months or so to [finish].

TYLER: [Nodding] Right, right. How does your voice fit into it? In "Good Potato Soil" and "Papermaker Pride," that first-person point of view is so intense, and distinguishes itself from the rest of the collection. For stories like that, did you start with the voice, or start with the content or premise and let the voice follow?

ELIOT: It usually starts with an image, and then I sort of struggle with the first page until I get a voice that sounds unique, or sounds right. I started the "Papermaker Pride" story when I was teaching a composition class, and [the students] had to write a reflective essay about some moment in their past, and I said "well, I'll do this with you." So it started out as non-fiction, because I did play for really crappy soccer team in High School that lost every game. [Both laughing]. Then I tried [the story] as fiction and that didn't work, then I tried it in the third-person and [finally] settled on first-person.

TYLER: Ah.

ELIOT: Third person just throws me. I cannot figure out how to write in third person, at all. So I think almost all of the stories in the collection except for two are first person. I think I just stick with first person because it's all I sort of know how to do, and I generally just like first person better. It just feels more intimate, more authentic.

TYLER: And I imagine on a project like this with a lot of the same ideas and subject matter, it's useful to lend the same subjectivity to the whole collection. You don't need to have one voice because you can get different people's input.

ELIOT: That's true. And I guess one thing I was always afraid of was that even with all these different characters, because it's in first person, it would sound the same. And some people have said that's not true, that each character has a voice.

TYLER: Oh, yeah.

ELIOT: Which was good to hear because that was a huge fear—[that I was] giving each character a different name but they [would] all have the same voice throughout all the stories.

TYLER: Yes. Well, you have the collection of stories coming out in the fall. [I'm wondering], do you have any thoughts on the state of the short story in American literature today?

ELIOT: I've read a lot of great short stories recently, and for a while that's all I read. I've never understood the reluctance to publish short stories. I don't know why they don't sell as well. I think they're coming back around to a certain degree, with small presses publishing them and with different venues, and with Steve Allman and Jim Shepard and all these different people writing great short stories. I want it to keep going, it's my favorite genre; I'd rather read a short story collection than a novel, to be honest.

TYLER: [Nodding] Right, right.

ELIOT: So, I hope it stays strong, because I have a book to sell. [Laughter].

TYLER: Let's talk about that. Ooligan Press, they're a teaching press or student-run, is that what I was reading?

ELIOT: They're a teaching press, part of Portland State University and the Master's program in publishing and [writing]. I first submitted the collection to the University of Wisconsin-Stevens Point, and had my heart set on [their press] doing it. They're a little press, they're non-profit; and although I think every writer wants to get the big publisher and be on Oprah and all that. [Both laughing]. And I definitely want that, there's something in me that likes the idea of a student press where the students are learning and being part of it. The UW press did not accept my book and I felt pretty heartbroken, and at that point I was pretty close to giving up. I had submitted my book to a bunch of collections, sent it out to agents, had gotten feedback [such as] "we really like this but the stories are very quiet and we don't think it's going to work." At the sort of moment of deepest despair where I was [thinking] I was going to quit and give up, I kind of stumbled across Ooligan and they ended up being the press that took it. I really appreciate working with them because I went to Presby College as an undergrad, and part of that was really experiential learning with a lot of practicum courses, like working on a journal with other students and learning by doing. I really appreciate that both as a teacher and a writer, so I'm glad that it ended up at Ooligan. [I appreciate] that it's part of a learning process, and that it's not just about me, but also about them learning how to do it. They've also taught me a lot about the publishing industry, how to do marketing, and things like that, so I've learned a lot actually.

TYLER: Yeah. [Nodding]. That sounds really cool. So, you live in Oregon, is that right?

ELIOT: Yeah, I live in Eugene.

TYLER: Has that influenced your writing at all? Is [Eugene] different or similar to northern Wisconsin?

ELIOT: It's both similar and different in a lot of ways. I don't know that it's influenced my writing so much yet, as far as style and things go, but I do think it was necessary for me to leave Wisconsin in order for me to write about it. I looked at a map recently and noticed Eugene and northern Wisconsin are about the same latitude.

TYLER: I wouldn't have guessed that!

ELIOT: At one point Northern Wisconsin was like the northwest of the United States. There is something similar. I haven't traveled that much, but of all the places I've ended up it's the first one that's kind of felt like home, the way Wisconsin has felt like home. There are a lot of Wisconsin folks out here for some reason.

TYLER: Is there anything you want your readers to take away about that area from reading your book? Is there one thematic feel that you want them to get about that region?

ELIOT: Hmm. Good Question. [Both laughing]. I love the quote at the beginning of the book from Glenway Wescott: "It resembled the meanest poverty but it was actually quite wonderful." So that there are these hidden spots, not just in northern Wisconsin but throughout rural America where it looks really desperate and rundown, but it's actually quite rich; there's community there, there's diversity, the landscape is both a burden and something that gives the place life. One thing about Wisconsin, and maybe this applies to western Oregon, too, where it's grey and rainy for eight months out of the year, is that Wisconsin is very beautiful but it's also very flat and muted, and has harsh winters, so there's this attitude of enduring; and I think that's the thing I want to speak to, is the idea of perseverance and enduring. Maybe it's my Lutheran upbringing of sucking up, and trudging on even though it's crappy and cold out, and finding a way to go on.

TYLER: It's funny, when I read your book, Wisconsin was considered another "flyover" state, and just this week it's been all over the news and on the front page! [Laughter]. Recall aside, it seems like it's kind of a microcosm of a lot of division going all over the country, and I was wondering if what's been in the news the last week means something to you, or if it sheds new light on the place you grew up?

ELIOT: I don't think I ever thought of Wisconsin as a progressive state. When I was growing up, I thought it was the most conservative place ever, but as I grew up and moved and matured, I realized that there was this long progressive tradition. It's really interesting; it's the place where collective bargaining started, all the Leopolds, Earthface started there. But it's also the place where the John Birch Society started, and McCarthy was from Wisconsin, so there are radical differences. What's interesting to me is that Wisconsinites are so polite; they're not into yelling at one another. I was at a conference and a woman there told a story of what exemplified midwestern manners to her, and this story always stuck out to me: she was at a restaurant with someone who ordered a grilled cheese sandwich, and when the sandwich came it had a very clear bite taken out of it, but the customer would not send it back—because that was not the polite thing to do, to make a fuss.

TYLER: [Laughter].

ELIOT: I don't know what's going on in Wisconsin right now, sometimes I'm at a loss as to why people vote the way they do. The world overwhelms me at times.

TYLER: [Laughter] Yes. So what are you working on next, as far as writing goes?

ELIOT: I'm working on a couple things. One is this essay about the desks I've had over my writing career and the different methods I've had. You asked about my process, and when I first started writing I had so many habits; for instance I had a word processor and I would set up my boom box on top of it with the speakers pointed at me, and would always have to have music on. And then for a while it was like I could only write in the dark with candles put around me, all sorts of stupid stuff like that...

TYLER: [Laughter].

ELIOT: Now the best thing for me would be the computer in the middle of nowhere, with no noise and no one around me.

TYLER: [Laughter]. No longhand?

ELIOT: I did go through a longhand phase, for sure! But I can't read my handwriting now, so now it's all computer. I've [also] been working on a young adult novel, about a canoeing trip that goes awry. That's stalled in the last couple of months, [because of] teaching. And I haven't written short stories for over a year, but I have a couple of ideas floating around, that I will come back to. That's part of my process too—I have an image or an idea, and I just keep thinking about it and thinking about it until I'm ready to sit down and write. That seems to go much smoother than sitting down right away as soon as I get an idea or image. That never works for me; I just stall out right away.

TYLER: Great, well thank you!

photo by Todd Cooper

Eliot Treichel is a native of Wisconsin who
now lives in Eugene, Oregon. He holds an MFA
from Bennington College and currently teaches
writing at Lane Community College. His work
has appeared in *Beloit Fiction Journal*, *CutBank*,
Passages North, and *Southern Indiana Review*.
Close is Fine is his first book.

CLOSE IS FINE is set in Adobe Caslon Pro, at 10.5 points, with 14 points of lead. Helvetica Neue LT Std is used as an accent and on the cover, at various point sizes depending on context.

Ooligan Press

OOLIGAN PRESS IS a general trade publisher rooted in the rich literary tradition of the Pacific Northwest. A region widely recognized for its unique and innovative sensibilities, this small corner of America is one of the most diverse in the United States, comprising urban centers, small towns, and wilderness areas. Its residents range from ranchers, loggers, and small business owners to scientists, inventors, and corporate executives. From this wealth of culture, Ooligan Press aspires to discover works that reflect the values and attitudes that inspire so many to call the Northwest their home.

Acquisition Team
Lauren Adam
Irene Costello
Rachel Haag
Kaija Maggard
Amber May

Project Managers
Katie Allen
Irene Costello
Rachel Haag
Marc Lindsay
Kaija Maggard

Design Team
Rachel Haag
Kelsey Klockenteger
Krys Roth
Mandi Russell

Cover and Interior Design
Tristen Jackman (Cover)
Jessica Snavlin (Interior)
Krys Roth (Interior)

Editing Managers
Kristen Svenson
Amreen Ukani

Editing Team
Katie Allen
Kathryn Banks
Irene Costello
Heather Frazier
Laura Gleim
Marc Lindsay
Isaac Mayo
Mandi Russell
Jonathan Stark

Marketing Managers
Emily Gravlin

Marketing Team
Katie Allen
Rachel Haag
Marc Lindsay
Kaija Maggard
Brittany Torgerson

OOLIGAN
P R E S S

Ooligan Press is a general trade publisher rooted in the rich literary tradition of the Pacific Northwest. A region widely recognized for its unique and innovative sensibilities, this small corner of America is one of the most diverse in the United States, comprising urban centers, small towns, and wilderness areas. Its residents range from ranchers, loggers, and small business owners to scientists, inventors, and corporate executives. From this wealth of culture, Ooligan Press aspires to discover works that reflect the values and attitudes that inspire so many to call the Northwest their home.

Founded in 2001, Ooligan is a teaching press dedicated to the art and craft of publishing. Affiliated with Portland State University, the press is staffed by students pursuing master's degrees in an apprenticeship program under the guidance of a core faculty of publishing professionals.

369 Neuberger Hall
724 SW Harrison Street
Portland, Oregon 97201
Phone: 503.725.9748
ooligan@ooliganpress.pdx.edu
ooliganpress.pdx.edu

Ordering Information

Individual Sales: All Ooligan Press titles are available through your local bookstore, and we encourage supporting independent booksellers. Please contact your local bookstore, or purchase online through Powell's, Indiebound, or Amazon.

Retail Sales: Ooligan books are distributed to the trade through Ingram Publisher Services. Booksellers and businesses that wish to stock Ooligan titles may order directly from IPS at (866) 400-5351 or customer.service@ingrampublisherservices.com.

Educational and Library Sales: We sell directly to educators and libraries that do not have an established relationship with IPS. For pricing, or to place an order, please contact us at operations@ooliganpress.pdx.edu.

Alive at the Center

{Portland} {Seattle} {Vancouver}

poetry | $18.95 | 178 pages | 5½" x 8½" | softcover
ISBN: 978-1-932010-49-7

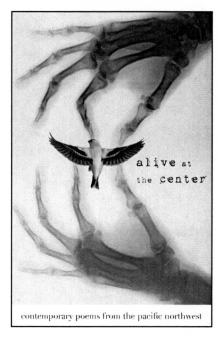

contemporary poems from the pacific northwest

Available March 2013 from Ooligan Press

The Pacific Poetry Project's first volume, *Alive at the Center*, aims to capture the thriving poetic atmosphere of the Pacific Northwest. It concentrates on the three major cities that define it—Portland, Seattle, and Vancouver, B.C. This anthology, compiled and edited by an outstanding poet from each city, is a cultural conversation among the unique urban communities whose perspectives share more than just a common landscape. *Alive at the Center* features distinctive, contemporary poets who speak to the individual spirits of these Pacific Northwest cities.

Also available as a three volume set

Alive at the Center
Poetry from the Pacific Northwest

Available March 2013

poetry | $9.95 | 5.5" x 8.5" | softcover

Portland

ISBN: 978-1-932010-57-2

The Pacific Poetry Project's
first volume, *Alive at the
Center*, aims to capture
the thriving poetic
atmosphere of the Pacific
Northwest. It concentrates
on the three major cities
that define it—Portland,
Seattle, and Vancouver,
B.C. This anthology,
compiled and edited by
an outstanding poet from
each city, is a cultural
conversation among the
unique urban communities
whose perspectives
share more than just a
common landscape. *Alive
at the Center* features
distinctive,contemporary
poets who speak to the
individual spirits of these
Pacific Northwest cities.

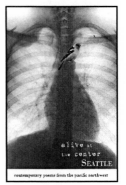

Seattle

ISBN: 978-1-932010-55-8

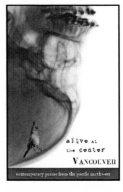

Vancouver

ISBN: 978-1-932010-53-4

OOLIGAN
PRESS

Up Nights

a novel

Daniel Kine

fiction | $14.95 | 200 pages | 5" x 8" | softcover
ISBN: 978-1-932010-63-3

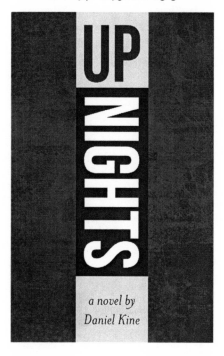

Available May 2013 from Ooligan Press

OOLIGAN
PRESS

Up Nights is a classic road novel for a new generation. Kine uses direct, unrelenting prose to tell the semi-autobiographical story of Arthur, a college-aged American male navigating his fractured existence alongside a childhood friend, Francis, their one-time mentor, Bill, and Bill's on-again-off-again girlfriend, Vita. They seek experiences that make them feel alive, struggling through empty relationships, their own addictions, and brushes with the law.

Survival League

Gordon Nuhanović

fiction | $10.95
104 pages | 5½" x 8½" | softcover
ISBN: 978-1-932010-06-0

In *The Survival League*, Gordon Nuhanović delves past Croatia's post-war politics and focuses on the people struggling to heal old wounds and create new lives. With edgy, evocative prose, Nuhanović weaves darkly optimistic tales where nothing ever works out quite right. Caffeinated punks, male pattern baldness, and Jehovah's Witnesses are all part of the lives the characters observe or reclaim. Through Nuhanović's natural storytelling voice, we hear the stories of survivors, not only of war, but of life and its spectrum—from the mundane to the insane. Already a hit in Croatia, *The Survival League* won the Society of Croatian Writers' Nightingale Award and the Ivan and Josip Kozarac Award. The Croatian daily newspaper *Jutarnji List* even voted it one of the top five books published in 2002. With the help of Croatia's Ministry of Culture, Ooligan Press proudly introduces this acclaimed storyteller to the United States.

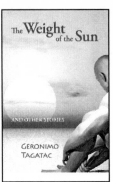

The Weight of the Sun

Geronimo Tagatac

fiction | $14.95
176 pages | 5½" x 8½" | softcover
ISBN: 978-1-93-2010-11-4

The Weight of the Sun, a short story collection by Geronimo Tagatac, sparkles with an appeal that comes from a deep understanding of human nature. Here are the farm laborers, dancers, kitchen workers, and soldiers who make up a world that is wrought with pain, nostalgia, and stunning grace. From the widowed Filipino father raising a son in a migrant work camp to the young veteran haunted by the ghost of war, *The Weight of the Sun* shows us not only what it is to be human, but how the human spirit can grow when faced with overwhelming adversity. Tagatac brings these characters home in our hearts with a poise and dignity that marks a new and powerful voice in short fiction.

You Have Time for This

Mark Budman & Tom Hazuka, Editors

fiction | $11.95
135 pages | 5" x 7½" | softcover
ISBN: 978-1932010-17-6

Love, death, fantasy, and foreign lands, told with
brevity and style by the best writers in the short-
short fiction genre. *You Have Time for This* satiates
your craving for fine literature without making a
dent in your schedule. This collection takes the
modern reader on fifty-three literary rides, each one only five hundred words
or less. Mark Budman and Tom Hazuka, two of the top names in the genre,
have compiled an anthology of mini-worlds that are as diverse as the authors
who created them. Contributing writers include Steve Almond, author of *My
Life in Heavy Metal* and *Candyfreak*; Aimee Bender, author of *The Girl in the
Flammable Skirt*; Robert Boswell, author of five novels, including *Century's
Son*; Alex Irvine, author of *A Scattering of Jades*; L. E. Leone, who writes a
weekly humor column about food and life for the *San Francisco Bay Guardian*;
Justine Musk, author of dark-fantasy novels, including *Blood Angel*; Susan
O'Neill, writer of nonfiction and fiction with a book of short stories, *Don't
Mean Nothing: Short Stories of Vietnam*; Katharine Weber, author of several
novels, her most recently *Triangle*. From Buddha to beer, sex to headless
angels, there's a story here for everyone. In *You Have Time for This* you will
find: flash fiction from forty-four authors, works from across the globe, highly
regarded authors from all types of genres, fresh work from emerging writers,
and fifty-three stand-alone pieces that tie the world together.

Enjoy. You have time for this.

**"A really good flash fiction is like a story overheard at a bar—personal, funny,
dangerous, and sometimes hard to believe. *You Have Time For This* distills
those qualities and many others into quick tall tales by writers who are as
talented as they are magical."**
—Kevin Sampsell, author of *A Common Pornography*
   and publisher of Future Tense Books

CPSIA information can be obtained at www.ICGtesting.com
Printed in the USA
BVOW021905030912

299358BV00002B/1/P